WHERE THE WIND CAN FIND IT

WHERE THE WIND CAN FIND IT

STORIES

Ben Nickol

Queen's Ferry Press
8622 Naomi Street
Plano, TX 75024
www.queensferrypress.com

"Flamingo Motel" originally appeared in *Fugue* (Issue 47, fall 2014)
"Missing" originally appeared in *CutBank* (Issue 82, spring 2015)
A version of "Like Gloves of Air" originally appeared as "Safe" in *Boulevard* (Issue 89, spring 2015)

Published 2015 by Queen's Ferry Press

Cover design by Brian Mihok

First edition November 2015

ISBN 978-1-938466-50-2

Printed in the United States of America

For my parents

CONTENTS

AS IF ANY MOMENT

THE ONLY GAMBLER IN MY LIFE, that I knew of, was an uncle no one talked about. Lyle was his name, my mom's stepbrother. He's actually still alive, though I could pass him in the street and not know it. When I was a girl, and someone mentioned Lyle, there was sighing and knotted jaws. He was what I learned in parochial school was called prodigal, though he never came back, or hasn't yet. All I knew about him, and all I know still, is he gambled. At some point I developed an image of him. He sits at a felt table in a room completely dark except for the lamp over the table, with only his lips (out of which hangs a cigar) visible under the brim of his hat. He wears suspenders, a collared shirt. Around him are cards, chips, whiskey. Or his hat's cocked to the side, his sleeves are rolled, and he's at the track, thumping his program on the rail while a pack of hounds flies through the stretch. This was my Lyle, and more importantly this was my gambler. Gamblers were a species, identifiable on sight. They weren't young guys fresh out of school, weren't boys with neat hair and deep dimples whose eyes, when they smiled, filled with worlds you didn't see but wished to.

I met Kevin at a bar. This was in Chicago. I was twenty-three and, like everyone twenty-three, lived in Lincoln Park, that jungle gym of young professionals. You had your degree and first job, your apartment, and every evening you came down from the tracks at Armitage or Fullerton, the train thundering overhead, and walked into the streets. There was long light, I remember that. Light stretched from the trees even after dusk had darkened the sidewalks. You went with your friends to bars. The place I met Kevin had tall booths and English lamps, and was crowded most nights, including the night this lean boy in a sweater vest and checkered shirt, utterly alone, slid into our booth and dropped his palms on our table. He looked, in turn, at each of us, four or five girls sipping drinks and hoping to seem equal parts alluring and uninviting.

"Yes?" Kinzie said. She was a bitch.

"How're things, girls?" the kid said.

"We don't need your assistance, if that's what you're wondering."

He looked at her. "You have a sour heart," he said.

"What?"

"Your world view. It's appalling." He looked at the rest of us. "Is this how she is?"

It was, though none of us confirmed it.

"God, are you all this way?" He looked at each of us, and seeing what he needed to see, or not seeing it, rapped the table. "Well, good luck." He walked off.

When he was gone, Kinzie said, "What a fag."

"Total fag," said Marie, who was Kinzie's lieutenant.

The committee had spoken on the matter of Sweater Vest. A verdict had been reached. We ordered drinks and said mean things about other people in the bar, or people we knew. That would be our night, because that was our night most nights. It was our pattern. All that changed were the outfits we wore, and the bar, and those didn't change much.

I guess my attention drifted. That's how I remember it. Kinzie was talking, describing a ho she worked with who had gross cleavage. Her tits, she said, were twenty inches apart. They looked like skis. My gaze floated through the bar. I wasn't looking for anything in particular, just something else, something new, and what I saw, eventually, was Sweater Vest. He sat by himself, talking to the bartender. He leaned on the counter, watching the man's mouth as if at any moment something miraculous would fly from it, a dazzle of light or wild bird.

He still was there when we left, nodding at each word the man said. I couldn't imagine what could be so engrossing. We were going elsewhere. There'd be guys, Marie said, though of course guys were everywhere and all we did was roost like buzzards.

"Think I'm headed home," I said.

"What?"

"I'm pooped."

"You're such a ho," Kinzie said. But they hugged me and walked off. It was a quiet night, a pale light filtering down from the tracks. When they rounded the corner, I went back in.

He hunched so intently at the bar that his vest hiked up his back. He had a foot on the lath of a stool, as if he'd climb over the bar and into the bartender's mouth. I tapped his shoulder.

"What? Oh, hey!" he said.

"Hey."

"I know you. You're from the, uh…" He snapped his fingers.

"Sorry about that."

"The ice brigade, yeah. No worries."

I didn't know what to say. "You seem fun," I said.

"Yeah? Well, we can work with that."

I had a feeling then that I'd have often with Kevin, for years. Something bloomed from him, or was soon to bloom, some world with slanted rules he'd wrap over me like a quilt. It inspired a kind of helpless levity, like laughter of the blood, and would be a feeling I remember fondly except that Kevin himself believed new and better worlds would bloom from him, and that proved a sad thing for him to believe.

"Let's have a drink," he said. Then, our drink finished, he said, "Let's go."

We went outside and up the sidewalk. It was early, maybe eight or nine. You could leave with a guy at eight or nine and not have it mean anything, though from the start, with Kevin, I was happy to have it mean something. The way he walked, with his light strides, getting ahead and walking backwards while I caught up, before skipping around and floating forward again, and how he talked, using a hand only to punctuate certain points before stuffing it away in his pocket, as if this tremendous thing inside him would escape if he weren't careful—something drew Kevin, some magic beyond seeing, and if I stayed nearby I might find magic too.

"Where're we going?" I said.

"We're almost there." He touched his ear. "You hear it?"

All I heard was a car alarm, and somewhere a train clacking into a station.

"You have to feel it, too. Let yourself feel it," he said.

It was a way he never stopped being. Even later, when we were settled and in the stride of things, and it was everything I had to wake up and get through a day, Kevin would feel something, suddenly, and be off chasing it. It could be irritating, though also was miraculous. Once he made a guitar with tools from the garage, and once he decided he'd learn Czech. The CDs came in the mail, and soon he was speaking it around the house. *Muj trepetavy ptak*, he called me, his fluttering bird.

At the end of the block, in a brownstone with a broad stairway mounting from the curb, we found a party. In every window stood people with strange hats. Hats were the theme, evidently. People in strange hats exited a cab. Other hats smoked cigarettes on the sidewalk. These Kevin waved to, shouting hello.

"You know them?" I said.

"These guys? No." He yelled to them, "Hey, we'll get our hats!"

He led us down the street, studying the dark houses he passed, as if looking for a specific shop, for a milliner's. And he found one, wouldn't you know, or what worked for one. He opened a little gate and entered someone's garden.

"What're you doing?" I said.

"What color are your eyes?"

"What?"

He glanced back. "Blue? Got to be blue. Ice brigade."

"Someone's watching," I said.

The house was dark, but a curtain had parted and a bald guy in sweats was peering down at us. Kevin lifted a hand. Reluctantly, the man waved back.

"Just two." Kevin held up two fingers.

The guy's hand went to his ear.

"Two!" Kevin shouted. "No more, I swear. And maybe some of your bush."

The guy couldn't hear, or heard perfectly and didn't understand. He waved us on anyways.

"Thank you!" Kevin shouted.

The curtain fell.

Proceeding, he tore a branch from the bush and brought it to me. "That work?" He looped the branch and placed it on my head. "There. Roman-style."

I touched the garland as if it were a tiara. I actually still have that thing somewhere. I'll never get rid of it.

"Now..." He browsed through the flowers, some poofy hydrangeas, and snapped off a pair, one violet and one a pale, almost glowing blue. He tucked them in my garland, so they bobbed like antennae. I felt ridiculous, but it was the kind of ridiculous rare and dignified birds must feel, more elegant than silly. "Thanks," I said.

He studied his work. "Beautiful," he said.

Without thinking—because that's how it was with Kevin, each next moment was whatever you wanted or believed—I leaned forward and kissed him. I kissed his cheek, then moved and kissed his mouth.

"Well," he said.

I kissed him again, harder.

"Not bad," he said, "not bad. I knew this was my night."

"Yeah?"

He kissed me, just a quick one, and returned to the bush. That was the thing with Kevin. It always was some next thing, whatever was fresh and bright. He made himself a hat, like mine but smaller, and we attended the party.

I don't remember it. A crowd of laughter and hats, I suppose. At the end of the night, we climbed from an upstairs window and drank wine on the roof. All around us were trees stuffed with insects, beyond which hung the glow of downtown. "What should we do?" I said.

"I don't know. It's all right there."

What we did, it turned out, was go to his place. He lived north, in some neighborhood I didn't know. The next morning was fragrant and warm. We walked farther north, through neighborhoods neither of us knew, and ate breakfast at a diner with green walls. After that we lived together, and after that got married and had kids and moved to Colorado, all of these Kevin's ideas. Always, it was his ideas that sailed us on.

In the twelve years I knew him, between that night in Chicago and the night he drove to Ignacio, where the casino was, and then kept driving to the motel in New Mexico, where he wrapped the clothesline around his neck—in all those years, I only once saw Kevin gamble. We were driving through Montana. He'd decided we should see Glacier and Yellowstone. At a gas station outside Livingston (all the gas stations in that state have video poker), he fed a twenty in the slot and lost it in two minutes. He produced another and lost that, and hesitated only a moment before knuckling the machine and pushing off his stool. He drew a breath, "Hey, it's fine, right? No worries." And it was, it was fine. Walking to the car, he looked fresh and awake, the wind in his hair.

When they found him, there was so much confusion. No one had suspected anything. When it turned out there was no money, and in fact less than none, there was on the one hand less confusion, and on the other hand more. My parents hired a lawyer, not because things could be fixed but because we needed to know.

It turned out he'd always gambled. We didn't, and still don't know, what kind of gambling, but as far back as the lawyer could get records for there were cash withdrawals, big ones, from ATMs at casinos in Colorado, Arizona, other places. One withdrawal, from a bank in Las Vegas, totaled three-thousand dollars. I didn't know he'd ever been to Vegas. The lawyer gave me dates, but they meant nothing. Occasionally he'd left town for work, or what I was told was work. I guessed it was then.

The lawyer came around the desk to where my parents and I sat. He had a legal pad and pen. "I won't make this fancy. I doubt you want that. But how it looked..." He sat on the desk with the pad on his knee, as if instructing kindergarteners. From the left side of the page to the right, he drew an upward-sloping curve. "The withdrawals got bigger, and more frequent." He drew a second curve starting where the first had started, but sloping down. "The balances shrank. What you see in the middle," he drew squiggles between the two curves, "that's what you call trouble."

When we didn't say anything, he tapped the bottom curve. "When that hit zero," he tossed the pad aside, "that was bad trouble."

"Honey?" my dad said.

He sounded far-off.

"Sweetie?"

Someone brought me water, and for a time everyone hovered. They thought I was worried about the money, but obviously I was broke, I already knew that. What was torture was knowing Kevin had come this way. This was the path he'd taken. He was just ahead, it seemed, around the bend. If we hurried we'd catch him. Except he'd already arrived, at the Skyview Lodge or wherever. I wish they'd never told me the name of that place.

"This isn't easy, I know," the lawyer said.

"Let's keep going," I said.

He shifted on the desk and continued.

At first, Kevin had just used credit. He took out three or four cards, and when further applications were denied took out cards at higher rates, fringe cards from obscure companies. The cash we needed, for the mortgage and car payments, had come from our paychecks. But what was left of the checks, plus the cash advances he got on the cards—all that disappeared. There simply was no record of it. The lawyer said we could solicit surveillance from the casinos, if we wished, but he didn't see the point.

"You mean like tapes?" I said.

"Surveillance, yes."

"So we'd watch him lose money? Why?"

"As I said, I don't see the point."

When I had nothing to add, the lawyer studied some papers. "Now my hunch is that..." They were the wrong papers. He studied others. "MasterCard ending in 6632? This was yours?"

"I think so?" I said.

He laid the papers aside. "It was the only of yours with pragmatic spending. And the oldest."

"Wait," I said. "Only of mine?"

"This may come as a shock..."

"We're past that," I said.

"Of course." He shifted on the desk. Then he explained: with his own cards maxed, and with applications for further cards denied, Kevin had taken cards in my name. He'd not, at that point, used the kids' names. The lawyer was clear on that. Instead, when the cards in my name were maxed, he'd raided our retirement, and at last leveraged the house. The house money had lasted awhile. Most of it had sat in a bank I'd not heard of. "This was two years, nearly three," the lawyer said, shuffling some papers. When the house money was gone, he'd applied for a third mortgage, but was denied. That's when he'd taken cards in the kids' names.

The lawyer didn't know when Kevin's dealings with brokers had started. If he had to guess, there'd been bets, and heavy bets, when Kevin had had the house money. If he'd made good on those, as he could've then, he would've earned credit with the brokers for heavier bets, bets he couldn't make good on. But he'd been dealing with brokers, the lawyer was pretty sure. There were transfers to offshore accounts.

My dad was confused. "Brokers? What's a...I don't understand."

"It's like a bookie and payday lender, balled in one. Not very legal." The lawyer sighed. "And I'm afraid not good people to deal with."

Something occurred to me then, something I wanted not to know, but had to. "When?" I said.

"Pardon?"

"When was this?"

"As I said, it's hard to..."

"You said there were transfers. Offshore something. When was that?"

He looked at the papers. "The last one was last year. But the transfers, actually, in terms of his dealings—that's not the thing to know. Any, uh..." He twirled a hand. It was clear he had the word he needed, but sought another. Finally he gave up. "Any threats, or anything—not that I think there's a threat now..."

"Would've been later," I said.

For just a moment, he wasn't a lawyer. He dropped his hands. "Later. Yeah."

"Honey?" my dad said.

I wasn't the widow you hear about, who can't cry then does, suddenly. I'd been crying all along. And there I was again. The lawyer offered tissues and excused himself. My parents closed in. "I know, honey, I know," my mom said. "It's hard to understand."

Only she didn't know. And actually I did understand. As of that moment, I understood.

Earlier that year, maybe three months before he'd driven to New Mexico, Kevin had come home from work, or what I'd assumed was work (learning what I've learned, every minor detail is dubious, only a few key facts are certain), and said Durango was no place to be, not in January. This was strange. Kevin loved to ski and loved his Saturdays snowshoeing Hermosa Creek (though I understand now, of course, not every and perhaps not even many of those Saturdays were spent in the woods). Why would we leave? Though in its way, it wasn't strange. This was Kevin. For my husband, tomorrow wasn't governed by today.

He threw his keys on the counter. "You know what I mean?"

I didn't, but I never knew what Kevin meant until he showed me. "Sure," I said.

"We need a vacation."

Sam, our youngest, came in the kitchen. He was carrying the Popsicle sticks he and Kevin had invented a game from. You batted them like batons (I never quite understood it). Kevin swept him into his arms. "That sound good to you, pal?"

"What?"

"Want to get on a plane?"

"Yeah!"

"We have to decide where we're going. Planes fly everywhere. We have to choose."

"Can I bring Simon?" It was his walrus.

"Does Simon like planes?"

"I think he does!"

Kevin set him down. "Well, go ask him."

When Sam was gone, he said to me, "You know what I mean? Let's get out of here."

"I'll go," I said. There were four or five times in my life I said that to him, four or five important times, and that was one, though in the end, as you can guess, we went nowhere. "Where're we going?"

"We've got the passports, right? For Eva and Sammy?"

"They're somewhere, yeah." We'd not been out of the country, but we had the passports. They were a gift from my parents.

I put on water to boil, and heated oil in a pan. I was making pasta, I remember. But when I crossed to the pantry, Kevin was standing there. "What?" I said.

"The passports?"

"*Now?*"

"We've got to go, babe. I'm itching."

"Okay, slow down," I said.

"Let's just go."

"Babe, this takes planning."

"Well, let's plan. What should we plan?"

The oil was burning, so I switched off the flame. "We don't even know where we're going," I said.

"Where do you want to go?"

"I hadn't thought about it, Kevin."

Eva came in.

"What about this one?" Kevin picked her up. "Where's she want to go?"

"Zimbabwe!" she cried. It was from one of her books.

"That's an option. Everything's an option. You want to ride a hippo? Tell you what, get that globe from Daddy's office. We're having a meeting."

"Family meeting!" she screamed, and ran through the house. She screamed it again, then screamed siren sounds.

Kevin laughed. "There you go. Africa."

"We're not going to Africa," I said.

"Call it a working thesis. What else, what are we planning?"

"There's work," I said.

"Talked to them this morning. And you said you had time coming."

"The house…"

"We'll pull the shades."

"What about school?"

"School's on the way to the airport. They should be open tomorrow. We'll swing by…"

"*Tomorrow?*" I said.

Sam ran through the kitchen. "Family meeting!"

Kevin switched off the other burner. "Let's go."

In the living room, we sat on the sofa with Eva and Sam and the old, brass-swiveled globe at our feet. The globe was one of Kevin's treasures. It'd been his grandpa's. But now he took a pen, a felt marker, and started crossing off countries. He started with the U.S. "So not here," he said, and drew an X from Maine to San Diego, Seattle to Key West.

"Babe," I said.

"And not here…" He crossed off Canada, then England and France, and finally all of Europe. Though Iceland was fine, he said. He circled Iceland. He eyed Australia, then crossed that out, and I guess to dry the ink spun the globe once, hard. When it stopped, he set it between Eva and Sam.

"Really?" Eva said.

"Up to you. But you have to agree."

They approached the globe tentatively, as if they shouldn't spook it.

"Hold on," I said, and took the globe in my lap. I took the marker from Kevin and crossed out the Middle East. I thought I was finished, but then crossed out Africa.

"Mom!" Eva screamed.

"Sorry, honey," I said, and gave it back.

There was some bickering, but eventually it was down to Chile, because it was like the food chili, and was skinny, Madagascar because the leg of my X didn't reach it, technically, and Papua New Guinea, because Sam liked guinea pigs. They debated the merits of each, and finally eliminated Chile. But when no consensus could be reached, Kevin took the globe back and said Chile it was.

"Da–ad!" they cried.

"All right, pack your stuff," he said. "You'd think it'd be cold there, but it's summer."

The kids were up and running around. Kevin looked at me. "Chile," he said.

"I guess so."

"Hey," he said. "I love you."

"I love you, too."

"I mean no matter what," he said.

He had more to say, I think, but then nodded and patted my knee. He went in his study, and when he came out later we had boarding passes. We went Albuquerque–Houston–Panama City–Santiago, and as it happened we wouldn't be stopping by the kids' school. The flight left at 6:00 AM, and Albuquerque was 250 miles away. We had to leave in four hours.

"When're we coming back?" I said, and he had an answer ready. "Two weeks," he said.

I suppose it's obvious to you, but not until the meeting with the lawyer did I realize it: Kevin wasn't planning a vacation. Knowing that, there were things I remembered about the night, little things that in the moment were lost on me, but that now were unmistakable. For instance, Kevin had packed pictures. I remembered it clearly, him stuffing them in the suitcase, one of us and several of the kids. He explained himself: "In case we lose our passports. They'll prove we're family," he said.

And once packed, he walked through the house. He was closing things up, he said, but that wasn't what he was doing. He left blinds open, lights on. Other trips we'd taken, he'd liked to leave a clean house, so that when we came home it was like arriving somewhere new, but there was clutter everywhere, and he didn't touch a thing. He looked at the rooms. Then he went in the yard. I remember I emptied a dustpan on the patio and saw him there, out at the farthest reach of the houselights.

"Hon?" I said.

He didn't hear me.

"Babe?"

He'd been looking at something, then saw me and came in. "Checking the vents," he said, and I just assumed that was something you did.

I hate remembering that night. Not because I know now what was happening, and where Kevin was going, but because I know everything that was in him then, and not in us. How distant he must've felt. The kids and I, we were going to South America. A continent had opened before us. Kevin tried to share that thrill—he told Eva there weren't hippos, but he'd catch her a sloth and maybe an anaconda—but for him Chile must've been only the narrowest, most desperate sliver of hope. How lonely he must've felt, swimming in his family's joy. I hate to think of us packing, our shoulders brushing as we walked back and forth in our room, and me just deciding which dresses to bring.

Though the part of the night I truly hate remembering came later, sometime after midnight. The kids were asleep, or at least in bed. We'd said we'd wake them when it was time. Meanwhile, we loaded the car. Kevin was in his manic state, loading two suitcases at a time, organizing the trunk methodically, like a game of Tetris. He brought out blankets and pillows, so the kids could sleep on the way. Lastly, wanting to warm up the car, he hit the button for the garage door.

Sometimes I think I made this up, the way we invent memories for parts of our childhood we know happened but couldn't possibly remember. But I don't think so. I remember this. The garage door lifted, and Kevin opened the car door. He was about to get in, but stopped. The car was backed in, so that standing there he was looking down the driveway. And something was out there, or someone. Where I was standing, I couldn't see great. But across the street, at the Marstons' curb, was a car. Someone was standing there.

Kevin didn't move. Then he shut the car door and walked in the house, closing the garage door behind him.

I found him in the kitchen. "Hey, you okay?"

He eased onto a stool.

"Babe?"

He looked terrible. But then he was himself again, beaming.

"You know, let's put it off."

"What?"

"Yeah, sorry, I just…I remembered something. But we'll go. We still have the tickets."

After a while, we unloaded the car. It's hard to explain, but it actually wasn't that strange. Sometimes Kevin had an idea, then it went away.

My father's not so graceful. When the meeting was over and we were leaving, he said to the lawyer, "But I still don't get it. He didn't have to…I mean bankruptcy, right? He didn't have to…?"

The lawyer looked at me before answering. I looked away. "The guys your son-in-law dealt with…" he said. He shook his head.

"I don't understand," my dad said.

"They don't recognize bankruptcy."

It took a while, but finally he got it. "Oh."

We walked to the car.

But I've never accepted that, not quite. They were bad people, I know. They would've killed him. But Kevin, and I'm not sure how to say this. Kevin wouldn't have gone bankrupt. That wouldn't have been an option. Not that he was proud. He was, but that wouldn't have stopped him. He just wouldn't have seen giving up and death as separate outcomes. I mentioned Lyle, my mom's stepbrother. After Kevin died, I thought I just was blind, and Kevin had been a Lyle, a hat in a dim room who'd managed to deceive me. The therapist I saw encouraged that line of thinking. She said, session after session, "It's hard when the people we love aren't people we know."

But what I told her in our last session, before I walked out and canceled all future appointments—what actually I screamed at her—was that was bullshit. I knew Kevin. More than anyone I've met or expect to meet, Kevin was what he seemed. He wasn't Lyle, or one of those people like Lyle, who wait at the Marstons' curb at night, seeking advantages, some narrow seam they can work to their profit. What Kevin sought—what he craved—wasn't workable numbers, but some magic beyond numbers, a life over which probability cast no net. I'm glad we didn't get the casino tapes. I couldn't have handled that. But I know, if we'd watched them, we'd have seen my husband at his tables, hovering in his chair, certain each next card afforded miracles no odds restrained. When no possibility of that remained, no Kevin remained. He and his miracles vanished in a single act. Bankruptcy? What would that've done? Signing the papers would've been just another clothesline. Afterwards, there'd have been no Kevin.

The Skyview Lodge along the San Juan River. I like to think he imagined it differently, that for my husband the night was an opening, a slipping at last into fresh realities, but all I know absolutely is by morning, when the maid found him, his imagining had stopped.

KNOTTED

MY ROOMMATE IN STILLWATER (they paired up the athletes) was an offensive lineman named Pudge, from Poteau, Oklahoma. We roomed together both years, before I top-tenned at the Valero Texas Open and just went right on to the Shell Houston Open the next weekend, and never returned to Stillwater, not even to collect my stuff. I liked Pudge. We fascinated each other, me being a tall, athletic specimen who'd never played a real sport, and he being a fatso who had. He used to come in at night and ask me, "You swing those sticks today?"

I'd tell him I had, and he'd set a chair by my bunk, where I probably was sketching trees (an old habit now, a new habit then). He'd sit with his knees packed in ice and one of those gallon-sized Gatorades, the kind with the plastic carrying handle, in his lap. "So you take those sticks. You swing 'em around," he'd say.

"And the goal's not to do it at all."

"That's what you were saying."

"The perfect round, mathematically, is without strokes. It vanishes."

"Quit blowing my mind, you dildo."

I'd sketch my trees, and Pudge'd sit there, contemplating golf. In those two years he told me probably sixty times he admired my sport over all others—over, as he put it, "other pursuits just generally"—though he'd personally never played, except once at the muni in Fort Smith, after which he'd vowed never to play again. He liked the sport because it made you smart (he thought I was smart because I sketched trees), as opposed to his sport, which he said made you dumber and dumber until you chewed a shotgun. He liked it because it was peaceful (I think the sketching again). Mostly, he liked it because you could play forever. Once, he looked over his shoulder from his computer. I saw on his screen a picture of Tom Kite holding his trophy after the 1992 Open at Pebble Beach. Kite was in his early forties then, but looked like a 90-year-old lizard.

"Could you beat this guy?" Pudge said.

"Not a chance."

He studied the picture—Kite with his dumb red sweater and librarian spectacles, leering at the camera like he might sneeze on it. Pudge said he wished he had a sport he could play forever. His greatest ambition was to make three years in the NFL, then buy fifty acres outside Poteau and raise hogs and hunt turkeys, or the other way around. Which is funny because we're twenty-seven now, Pudge and I, and I just read where he signed a six-year deal with most of it guaranteed. I'm the one who's a burnt-out shell of myself, and probably at risk for shotgun-chewing, though I wouldn't do something like that, though who thinks they would till they do? With my Tour money (I've still got a little), I bought a condo on Valley Lakes Golf Club in Spokane, Washington. It's occurred to me that Valley Lakes is my turkey farm in Poteau, though I try not to think of it that way.

I've finished playing for the day, nine holes and some work on the chipping green. I play every day, because Valley Lakes isn't my turkey farm, goddamn it. Twenty-seven is young. The PGA might be out of reach (your window at the Tour opens and closes, and you know when it's closed), but if I get my mind right I could play in Asia or Europe, or join PGA Tour Latinoamérica. It is a mind thing, deep down. I need to be total. I need to be the golfer I wish to see in the world.

I'm walking home (it's across eighteen and down the

seventeenth fairway), when I swerve inside and cross the pro shop to the lounge. It's complicated, my relationship with booze. I'm not an alcoholic. This isn't denial, either—I'm really not. I could quit today, and would quit if I thought I should, but where I need to get mentally is a place where I've abandoned myself to golf as a life, and am not holding back or hedging bets. Therefore, I need to be willing to drink. I need to accept drinking as part of my character, and not fret over it, just as Tom Kite accepts his lizard face. This is sounding more and more like denial, but trust me. One thing you learn on Tour, spending time with those guys, is the best ones could live or die, they don't care. They all drink and smoke and eat steak and fuck strangers. It's not that they want to die, it's that they've released the tiller and become themselves.

Or I'm a drunk, who cares. Marty, the gay kid who drives the snack cart, emerges from the kitchen with my Jim Beam. I carry it onto the patio, where the old guys, the lawyers, are relaxing in the sun. They like me, these lawyers, because I am (or was?) the real deal, and being near me validates them. I haven't decided whether I like them back, and am trying not to decide. Liking people one way or the other doesn't matter.

"Les," one of them says. "The incomparable Leslie."

I sit and prop my heels on a chair. "Boys."

"You drinking tonight?" one says.

"I don't know."

"We're on a bender. The clouds are gathering."

One of them, a beanpole named Albert (that's not his name, but I call him Albert because "Albert" comes to mind when I see him) puts down his beer and shows me his new grip. "It used to be like this…" He fiddles with his hands. Marty walks by and I order more bourbon.

"Now it's like this. Is that better?"

Nothing inside me wants out, so I don't speak. Albert drops his hands. It's around then the heads at the table all swivel towards something behind me, and follow its movement, like six telescopes tracking a single star. A girl my age or younger, or older (I've lost touch with my own age, which has shot my ability to gauge the age of others) appears at my side. "Hello, gentlemen," she says.

"What're you doing here?" says Albert.

"I was invited. You invited me."

"But you came," he says.

"Not very smart of me, huh?"

She looks at me, and I squint against the sun to see her. "Who's this one?" she says.

"You don't know?" one of them says. "He's a pro."

"Pro what?"

Someone explains. I see that she's blonde with bangs crowding her eyes, and the kind of face I'm not sure I like, which I like.

"Does being a pro mean your feet get a chair?" she wonders.

I'm not inspired to move my feet, but Marty arrives with my drink and freeing up the chair is part of my natural course of motion.

"Thank you," she says, and sits.

Marty touches her shoulder. "Honey, what can I get you?"

"What's he having?"

"Leslie?"

"Your name's Leslie?"

"He's a gem, trust me. He's drinking manly Southern bourbon."

"I'll have that."

The girl and I watch each other while Marty collects glasses, then look at Paul, who's talking. Paul's a Southerner, and the only of these lawyers I like. "Jenny, you're out of your mind coming here," he says. "We'll feed you to the lions. We are the lions."

"I needed a drink."

"Not with us you didn't. Jenny, it's suicide."

"I don't know." She eases back in her chair, and lifts her shades to the sun. "I like it here. I might join."

"That's a brave idea," Paul says.

"You're a lawyer?" I say.

She watches me from behind her shades.

"She's a lawyer, all right," Paul says. "But she's a pup. She's a lawyer like a puppy's a dog."

"With big feet," Albert says.

Paul says, "Big feet means you'll grow into something marvelous. It also means magnificent penis, in philistine circles."

The girl lifts an eyebrow at me, the brow slipping from behind her shades to behind her bangs like a modest thing slipping from robe to shower.

"You've got a penis?" I say.

She laughs, and Paul says, "Why if these two aren't already playing puppy games. Look at their puppy games!"

The sun falls, stretching shadows up eighteen, and one by one the lawyers check their phones and groan. They count money onto the table while Marty collects valet slips and trots to the parking lot. There was never going to be a bender. These men, and I pity them, lead a life between lives. They're one thing at happy hour, another at home and another at work, professing at each station that that's who they really are, until the horn blows and there's a shift change. I'll never be that way.

Jennifer and I (I've decided I'll call her Jennifer) have become their audience, sipping our bourbons while each complains about his wife and working weekends. Paul's the last to go. He's about to speak, then changes his mind and doffs an imaginary cap. He strolls into the night, swaying slightly. Now it's the two of us. I'm thinking Jennifer's about to leave, which I'm fine with, then decide I don't want her to leave, and trained as I am to follow the dictates of my character, I say, "Another drink?"

"Sure."

I look for Marty, and not seeing him I go inside to the bar. I pour the drinks and come back.

"He takes initiative," Jennifer says, swirling her glass. It's night now, and her shades are pushed in her hair. Her eyes are misaligned, just barely, though hard intellect shines through, and I'm reminded of a time I crashed a Maserati. It was in the bogs in Florida, where I lived, and I just sailed it into the swamp. I remember the machine twisted in the mangroves (a tree I draw frequently), all bent and steaming, with the halogen lamps shining through the night, cutting the steam and trees and clouds of insects. The connection is her irises, which are blue like the halogen was. "So you're a golfer," she says.

"Yes."

"How'd that get started?"

It's the question a psychiatrist would ask, if I decided my knots were too tight and I needed a shrink. But I am the knots, it's that simple. "I played golf. I always have."

"You must be good."

"That doesn't have much to do with it."

"No?"

"It's a disposition thing."

She thinks that over, or pretends to.

"You don't want to hear about this," I say.

"I don't?"

"What's being a lawyer like?"

She looks at her drink, then at the night beyond the patio. The only thing out there is the fountain in the lake. "It's boring. I hate it."

"Yeah?"

"You saw those guys. I'm going to do it, though."

"You're ambitious."

"It's just easier to decide you'll do it."

"Leslie *Niel*sen!" Marty says, sashaying through the tables. My last name's Foster, but Marty gets away with everything.

"What do you want?"

"You're *stealing* whiskey!"

"You were off with some dudes, Marty."

34

"Shut up, you shut up right now."

He sits in my lap and laces his fingers behind my neck, while I sit there waiting for it to be over. "So what do you think of this beast?" he asks Jennifer.

"He's not a lawyer."

"No, he *isn't*. And why do you guys hang out with those guys? I'm sorry, I just met you, I'm Marty." He unlaces his fingers and shakes her hand. "But those guys are obscene. Every night, it's faggot this, fag that. They're so tough when they're together, but one of them, and you didn't hear it from me, hangs around when it's dark and tries to fuck little bartenders." He's tapping his chest.

"Oh my God, who?" she says.

"Let's not. It's a good moment, we'll ruin it. Let's talk about this one." His hands return to my neck. "I like this one. He'd fuck me in broad daylight if he wanted to, he just doesn't."

"Nope," I say.

"But if you wanted to…"

"I don't."

"But if you did."

"Broad daylight," I say.

"See?" he touches his chest as if moved. "A gentleman!"

"Get off my lap."

He straightens my shirt and bounces to his feet. "If I were you, honey?" He touches Jennifer's arm. "It'd be a no-brainer."

He walks off, and she's smiling.

"That's Marty," I say.

She lifts her drink, but still is smiling and sets it down.

"What?" I say.

"What're you doing tonight?"

"I don't know."

"Where do you live?" she says.

"Me? I live here."

—

The night gives her a scent, a good scent, that pockets in the sheets. I'm breathing it, the room pale with dawn, then breathing her shoulder and neck and we're fucking again, her face pooled in hair so that a lip, softly bitten, is her only trace of expression. Afterwards, we're no more awake than we'd been. She turns her head and hair falls away. She watches me, then reaches for the stool I use as a nightstand. She's got my sketchbook. I don't want to show her the sketches, but they are what they are. She can do what she wants.

She leafs through them. "This isn't golf."

"Sure it is."

She stops at a cypress I drew up the coast from Riviera, after a Thursday that made clear I'd not be around Saturday, then turns the page to a locust. I don't know where the locust came from. She says, "How is this golf?"

I'm not inclined to tell her, but say, "Look at it."

"I am."

The locust is drawn in winter, wherever it is. The branches extend at sharp angles, each turn a joint, until a spear is reached, like lightning. It's a bouquet of dark lightning. "Start at the bottom," I say.

"Start?"

She's sitting beside me, the blankets drawn to her breasts, and I'm going to tell her what I mean. "The bottom," I say, and tap the base of the tree. "You feel that?"

"Feel it?

"It's going to grow. Feel it." I move my finger up the tree, not touching it so as not to smear the pencil. The trunk splits and I incorporate other fingers. My hand climbs, the fingers spreading. "Feel it pressing. Something presses down, but it presses up. Clear to the tips."

At the top, my splayed hand covers most of the branches. I drop it on her stomach.

"What presses down?" she says.

"Gravity."

"What presses up?"

I nod at the page. "The tree."

She studies the sketch, then turns it sideways and studies it that way. It's got to be seven or eight in the morning, and the locust is getting to me. I throw off the blankets.

"Where're you going?" she says.

"I'm golfing."

She lowers the sketchbook. I'm pulling a shirt from the closet. "Okay," she says.

This is hard, because I'm not mean and don't wish to be, but also I'm me, and nothing else. "I had fun," I say.

She's out of bed too, and hunting panties.

"I mean it."

She bundles the panties in her shirt and skirt, and on her way to the bathroom kisses my cheek. "Me too."

She leaves the condo before I do.

I have her number, and Friday after playing I text to find out her plans. I'm drinking on the patio, hoping the lawyers will show up and she with them. She texts back. Plans are in place, but I can come if I want. I set the phone in my lap and watch the sunlight glitter off the fountain, the tree in my chest growing limbs.

She collects me in her Lexus, wearing a cream-colored dress and black belt. I'm wearing what I've worn all day.

"Way to clean up," she says.

These are the moments to be yourself, center plumb, neither ceding nor attacking. The seconds wash over you. It's possible I should give up trees and draw boulders in rivers, unmoved by the current.

But Jen (I'll call her Jen now) doesn't care what I'm wearing. We haul out on Valley Parkway, then take I-90 into the sun.

Her friends are downtown, eating appetizers and drinking wine. They're carefully dressed, with features that shoot off like firecrackers when they spot us. Jen moves among them, kissing cheeks. In college, and then on Tour, I hated parties. I liked drinking and hated parties, and moments like these were why. No one has addressed me, and Jen's taking her time getting the cheeks kissed. I have nothing to do, and nothing to say. There's nowhere I can look, because if I look at a face that person will think I want to talk to them, and if I don't I'm staring at nothing. My solution back when was to produce my phone, or pick at a sleeve, and I could do that now except I don't care. I could stand in that lounge staring straight ahead for hours.

One of the guys decides he'll talk to me (he pivots in his chair), but I go to the bar for a bourbon. I come back and sit by Jen. "And this is Leslie," she tells them.

"Hello," I say.

"He's made sure he has a drink for himself."

I decide the drink is hers, and set it in front of her.

"Aw," someone says.

"But now I need one. Who needs one?"

No one does. I go to the bar, and when I come back they're discussing someone named Judith. A guy with fluffy hair says, "What I don't get is she's always on her phone. Who's she talking to? Have you talked to Judith on the phone? No one has. Yet every time she comes out…"

It could be the Queen of England talking, or the Dalai Lama. It has nothing to do with me, and so I sit with my bourbon, letting the words flow by. Eventually something's funny. The table erupts in laughter. I'd laugh with them, but the joke has no meaning, so I wear whatever expression I wore before the joke and stare at the air in front of me.

Fluffy Hair notices I'm not laughing, and explains. "You have to know Judith," he says. "She's so neurotic, but really she's sloppy. She just wishes she were neurotic."

"Yeah," I say. "I don't know her."

"Well that's…that's what I'm saying."

The table falls silent, but for me it's been silent. I've been sitting in silence since I got there. I sip my bourbon, letting the moment be the moment.

"But it's not like she's healthy, either," someone says.

"Judith?" Fluffy Hair says. "Well she's healthy, but doesn't want to be, which isn't healthy."

And they're laughing again.

When I go for more bourbon, Jen comes with me. We're standing at the mahogany bar (if there's one thing you see a lot of on Tour it's mahogany bars—I must've stood at five hundred of them), waiting for someone to help us. She says, "You know you don't have to be here."

"I want to be," I say, and I do. It's just that I don't want to become there.

"Well, you're not showing it."

"I don't know what to tell you."

The bartender arrives, and I order two bourbons. Jen says, "I'll get mine."

The bartender hesitates. "One bourbon," I say, and he pours it.

"If it's all right with you," she says, "I'm going to tell my friends to ignore you."

"Do you want me to leave?"

"No, I like you. You're…I don't know, you're steady. But they shouldn't have to babysit you."

"No one has to babysit me."

"That's what I'm saying."

We go back to the table and she gets everyone's attention. "Guys," she says, "let's be ourselves. Leslie, here. I like Leslie, but he's in his own world. He'll chime in if he has something to add. We don't have to include him."

They're all glancing at me, unsure what to do. I have nothing to say, and so should say nothing, but say, "She's right, you can relax. I'm fine."

I guess it works? It's not really my business whether it works. But the conversation starts again, and doesn't stop that I notice, and they order more appetizers and wine.

There's still light in the sky as Jen drives me home. She's not talking, though I don't get the impression she's mad. I'm not talking either, and I'm not mad. We pull into the condos. In the grassy area by the pool there's a party going on, with people in white shirts and big globes of light strung tree to tree. Some kids wave sparklers.

She puts the car in park. "Here we are."

"Do you want to come in?" I say.

She thinks about it, then shakes her head. "No."

I want to apologize, but nothing I've done I would've done differently. The other urge is to defend myself, but your actions are a house you live in, and if they need approval you're not really living there. "Okay," I say.

She watches the party through the windshield. "Don't think I don't get it. I get it, I'm the same way. It's just sad."

"I don't think it's sad," I say, and I don't.

She looks at me. "No? You don't ever want to...I don't know."

"What?"

"You don't want to give in?"

The question surprises me. "This is giving in," I say.

The kids chase one another with sparklers. Everything's fire and white cotton.

"Well, goodnight," she says.

Climbing the stairs to my door I get the impression she's watching me, but I look back and she's pulled into the street.

Standing over the ball, I understand myself as a machine that makes swings. I'm finely tuned. Two hundred yards off, a flag stirs in the breeze. I'm oriented to the flag, and to the breeze, but their presence in me is just that, an orientation, as a computer generating digital imagery is oriented to the ones and zeros of code. I let go, a kind of dying, and the swing forms. It's been there all along, that swing. My job is to remove obstruction and let it flow. There's a shape, a tempo. I ride within, neither pushing nor leaning back. It's over when it's over, not a beat sooner or later, and the ball's sailing, taking the wind and tracking the flag, but it's beyond me, my job's finished. I observe the shot with detachment, as a child might, or a bird.

I tap another off the stack, and assume my stance. I'm hitting well today, not because the balls are flying straight (they are, though I'm just dimly aware of that), but because I'm not interfering. The swings are frictionless, flowing back and through. Now and again I detect intrusion. I've gripped too tightly, or tried to guide the club, or power it. I've tried with my hands to engineer an outcome, rather than allow an outcome to flow from organic causes. But I detect it, and the next swing I abdicate control and the motion is natural.

I've said I'm not watching the shots, or I'm watching but don't care. That's true enough while the shots are good, but I start hitting poorly and those shots are hard to detach from. I block one right, then another, then spray one into the elms lining the range. I stand over the next ball and remind myself I'm an elm. I grow into swings. But if a natural motion is there, it's deeper than I can reach. I can't die all the way, and when I take the club back it's an awkward stick I drag with my hands. I have to guess where the swing path is, where it should stop and come forward, how fast I should go. The whole mechanism is a clumsy invention. I knife one into the trees.

I keep hitting, or trying to. Each shot I die as deeply as I can, but I can't die through the falseness. It's all false, and pretty soon I'm ready to cry. In a few years I'll be thirty, and it's suddenly so ridiculous that I've devoted my life not just to a game, but a game I'm not good at. All my commitment, my leaving college, my moving where no one knows me, with my regimens and solitude— all that becomes humiliating. I believed something about myself, without realizing that as soon as you have to believe it, as soon as you need convincing, it's a lie. The people who really have it (Pudge had it, for instance) don't struggle with it because they don't realize there's another way. They just are, and go where they go. They don't waste thirty years striking poses in their minds.

I should call her. I should shower and dress well, and drive to her house. I want to be what people are, which of course is what I am, what I've always been. I'll do what she says, provided she does some of what I say, and maybe we'll overlap enough to stick. We'll see what's ahead. But I'm still hitting, and soon I'm hitting well again, the balls sailing up the range. I'm deadened, ignoring the shots, not alert to anything.

I slip the club in my bag and am choosing another when the snack cart pulls up. "What's up, Lesbian?" Marty says. "Where's that girl?"

The sun's shining, it's breezy, and standing on the tee I'm a perfect thing, natural and light. I pull an iron, I don't know which, and tell Marty I want a bourbon. While he fixes it, I hit a stinger no more than twenty feet off the ground that lands and rolls forever. It'd get the job done in Ireland, where everything fights the wind, or in Japan, where the air's funny and I don't trust the grass.

MISSING

DUSK ARRIVED AT FOUR. The throngs jamming the chairlifts evaporated, revealing the corded lanes that all day had organized them. It was like the discovery of a skeleton. Below the village, down the road to town, the terraces of parking drained, revealing expanses of stained snow.

Claire, who hadn't skied that day but who nevertheless wore snow bibs and a parka, crossed from the hotel to the bar at the lodge. Luke, the bartender, came down the taps and flicked a towel at her. He poured her a beer.

"What's going on down here?" she said.

"It's a bar," Luke said, and set the glass in front of her before walking back to the kitchen. Sipping her beer, Claire studied the patrons at other tables, and some men playing pool. The bar's windows, all down the wall, were darkening slabs of ice. The men finished a game and started another, the balls lurching into the carriage. She walked over. "Who's the pro here?" she said.

"This guy," one of them said.

"Har-har," said his friend. He racked the balls. "You want to play?"

She shot a game with them. Between shots, she studied angles and options, but then stepped to the table and simply fired at the densest cluster, hoping commotion masked incompetence. The game finished, and something passed between her new friends. "We're headed out," one said. "Have a good one." And they drifted off.

She ate dinner at the bar, where Luke checked in on her. "I'm out of here," she told him. "I'm done with it. All of it."

He followed his wiping hand down the counter. When he returned, some minutes later, he said: "So what were you saying?"

"Fuck you."

She took her food to a table by the window, where a chill exhaled from the glass. She was still at the window when the night skiing came on, the lamps strung like pearls into the sky, through which floated skiers, just small shards of darkness chipped free and falling—and at the window when she saw, high above the night skiing, some lights all their own, floating oddly up the ridgeline.

And at the window when they came through the bar with the photograph.

They were ski patrol guys in red jackets with white crosses. They stopped at the first table and handed the photo around. She couldn't see it, but saw the sober way each person studied it, then passed it on, shaking his head. They brought it to Luke, then to her.

"Have you seen this girl?" one of them said.

She studied the photo. A girl in summer, standing in tall grass. "Who is she?" The photo was so warm. She doubted, on such a night, she'd recognize anyone photographed in sunlight and grass. She handed the photo back. "I'm sorry."

"If you see her, call the desk. All the phones 911 the desk."

"Andie," the other one said.

"What?"

"Her name's Andie."

When they left, the bar was still. The music, which before had gone unnoticed, now was a sharp, ugly presence, like a provocative sculpture. She went to the bar. "God," she said, but Luke was on the phone. Other people crowded around her. Finally Luke hung up. "They lost her," he said. "She went off the ridge."

"Jesus," Claire said.

"They're getting ready," said someone at the window. The

46

group of them, Luke included, left the bar and crowded at the glass. Below, under flood lamps, a team of riders ran checks on snow machines, their exhaust fogging the night. Before they left, one of them stood on his machine and addressed them through a bullhorn. He gestured at the mountain, finning a hand at their routes. Finally he climbed down and the riders, saddled in pairs on the machines, some with skis or snowshoes strapped to their backs, tore out through the dark.

Everyone had a drink, then Luke closed the bar and they went downstairs. The ski patrol office, behind its glass partition, was bustling, people zipping back and forth. Farther within, a cluster of officials consulted a vast topographical map. They weren't alone in convening there. People came in sweatpants and pajamas, or clomped down the stairs in boots. Luke talked to some guys from the kitchen, still in their breasted jackets. When he returned, Claire said: "We need to do something."

"Do what?"

"Do you know the patrol guys?"

"They don't need us, Claire."

Something was happening. Someone was pushing through the crowd. It was the guys she'd seen earlier, the guys with the photo. "Claire…" Luke said, but she stepped past him and blocked their way. "Hey," she said.

The men tried to step past her, but she got in front of them. "Hey," she said again. "I want to help."

"Ma'am," one said.

"I'm serious."

They tried again to step past her, but again she blocked their way. In the end, to appease her, they printed off some photos she could take around. She tried to find Luke, but he'd left.

For all the commotion in the lodge, it was a hushed, deserted night. The night skiing was off. Floating up the dark mountain, like phosphorescent bubbles, were the isolated stabs of snow machines' headlamps. She heard their engines, vaguely, but then was walking and heard only her own breath and crunching snow.

The hotel was dark, but she left photos at the desk and by the fireplace. A man crossed the lobby and she put one in his hand. "Her name's Andie. She's missing."

"Jesus," the man said, and she kept going. She left copies by the elevator and courtesy phones. After the hotel, she walked down the road, knocking at cabins and condos. Most of the doorways were dark, but where a door opened, she provided a photograph. "We've been looking since this afternoon. Any information…"

They were sorry to hear that, they said. "We need to find her. If you see her…"

If they heard something, they'd be in touch. They were sorry, they said.

She moved down the road. It was a cold night, but away from the village a milky light that was almost warmth descended through the pines. Below, in the valley, lay the shimmering lights of town. At the end of the road, an old couple answered in pajamas. The man fumbled glasses onto his nose. "What's this?"

"It's Andie. She's missing."

He held the picture away from him, then studied Claire over his frames. "If you see her, you need to call that number."

"We will," the man said.

"My name's Claire," she said.

When she returned, the room where the crowd had formed was vacant and dark. The only light came from the ski patrol office, where now a lone man stood at the map. Others sat at a table with papers and laptops. Stenciled on the door were the words STAFF ONLY, but in her hand were the rest of the photographs. She stood in the dark, rapping the sheets on her thigh.

When she entered the room, a woman looked up from the table. "Excuse me?" She lifted the pictures. "The fliers," she said. "Mike had me pass them out."

"Mike?"

It'd been a guess. Still, she kept on: "Are these not yours?" She brandished the fliers.

The woman studied Claire, then nodded at a shelf. Claire set the photos on the shelf, then waited, watching the woman work. "What can I do?" she said.

The woman again lifted her eyes. She folded her arms and sat back. "Who are you, again?"

"Mike had me help. He said to help."

"Anyone know a Mike?" the woman said.

There were shrugs. "Could be a Mike," someone said. "Could be with County."

"He said to help out. I'm helping out. What do we need?" Claire said.

"Look," the woman said, "we don't need…"

"Coffee? Anything like that?" Some heads lifted.

"What about food?"

"Or," the woman threw up her hands, "you could bring us some food. Sure."

Claire left and crossed to the hotel, where after bickering with a clerk and manager she was shown into the pantry. Everything she took—salads, sandwiches, breads—the clerk recorded and added to her room bill. When she returned to the office, carrying plastic bags and an urn of coffee, she was greeted like family. "There's our girl," one said. "Atta girl."

They circled like hyenas, peering in the bags. Once they were eating, she asked about the search.

"Nothing yet," one said.

"No?"

"It's a lot of land," another said. He was an older guy by the room's standards, a handsome guy. A radio crackled, and he unclipped it and jammed buttons. "Fucking thing," he said.

"So what do we do?" Claire said.

"We invest in radios. Fucking Soviet-era. Look at this thing."

"Let me see that," one of the young guys said, and the old guy tossed it to him. "Fucking radioshkinev," he said.

They ate awhile, chewing their food like cud, before the old guy stood and fed his arms into a jacket.

"Where're you going?" Claire said.

"Here," the woman said, "take them the weather." She handed the man a printout.

"Wait," Claire said, and pulled on her coat. She grabbed the coffee urn.

"No," the woman said. "You're staying here."

"No, I'm not," she said.

Any vehicle that could go up the mountain already had, but Charlie, the old guy, called a lift operator, who met them at the quad. It'd been frigid earlier, but now was arctic. The sky had cleared, releasing all fumes of warmth. They floated through the housing, then jumped cables and flew into the sky, each breath cutting her lungs.

It was a still night. Even soaring in the air things were still. Trees ghosted by, slumped in their wedding cakes of snow. What light there was emanated from the snow, from within, as if an overcast day had dropped from the sky and now smoldered on the mountainside. Stars shone above them, and to their left and right. The valley glimmered.

Charlie poured coffee. "Should you check in with Mike?" he said.

"Who?" she said.

He laughed. "Look, I don't care." He gave her a cup, then poured for himself. "I get it, I think. It's a good feeling."

"It's not about how it feels," she said.

"No," he said. "Of course not."

They floated up the mountain. As they neared the ridge, a wind kicked up, carrying grit that stung her eyes. The chair swung wildly. Within the blur, passing from view, were the floodlights and orange tent of the search party.

—

Inside, the tent was musty, and surreally lighted, as if it were surrounded by fires. There were tables and cots, and at the far wall a kerosene heater that looked like a cage for something radioactive. The walls sagged with wind, an icy draft leaking through. The two men in the tent stood when they entered, and conferred awhile with Charlie. They poured coffee without acknowledging where it'd come from. They studied the weather printout. Finally, one of them glanced at her.

"Oh," Charlie said. "And this is…" He snapped his fingers.

"Claire," she said.

"Claire. She's from County."

"You're not a monitor, are you?" one of them said. He was bald, with thin stubble where a tonsure would grow. "What, are they making us accountable?"

"That's what it sounds like," the other said.

"Unacceptable," the bald one said. "Unacceptable."

"I'm just helping out," she said.

"Well, that's fine. But let's keep that monitoring to a minimum. I'm Scott," he shook her hand, "and this is Sam."

From outside came the surging rip of engines, something like chain saws, and then abrupt silence. Two men ducked into the tent, covered in snow. "Wind's blowing!" one of them shouted into his helmet. Then they removed their helmets. "Hey," one said. "Who's she?"

Scott brushed them off. "That's our monitor," he said.

"They making us accountable?"

"Let's go," Scott said.

While the new guys unzipped, Scott and Sam zipped up. They pulled on gloves, took helmets from the rack. "Monitor?" Scott said, offering her a helmet.

"I'm going?"

"Got to find Andie, don't we? Yeah, you're going. Let's go."

—

In the floodlights, the snow was a whirling blindness, like sand infused with glare, but they soared off the ridge and soon the snow was confined to the machine's headlamp. She gripped Scott's torso, her chin at his ear. The headlamp passed over tracks, and caught in its scalloped periphery the low hang of timber. "Where're we going?" she shouted, but the helmet reverberated her voice. She doubted it went anywhere, and if Scott replied she didn't hear.

They followed a descending track, in the bend of which she saw, over her shoulder, the headlamp of the other machine. It was far back, drifting through the trees like a spirit. After a while, they arrived at a boundary rope. Scott stopped the machine, exhaust wafting forward, and lifted his visor. "You good?"

"Yeah," she said.

The other machine stopped beside them. "Do the basin?" Scott yelled, and Sam flashed his thumb.

Scott clapped his visor down and idled forward, lifting the rope over their heads. They went through a creek bed, then climbed out in timber. There was no path then, just snow. What had been a sturdy machine now wavered beneath them, like a kite. They ascended a ridge and she leaned with Scott's body. Dropping off the ridge, he leaned back against her. She watched trees pass over. In the ambience of their headlamp, the trees were like discovered things, their boughs shielding faces.

They crossed a meadow, the two machines in tandem, then angled off and killed the engines. Sam tossed them snowshoes, each shoe thumping the powder, then dropped his own and stepped on.

"You used these things?" Scott said.

"Yeah."

"They're pretty easy."

"I've used them," she said.

The shoes were steel hoops with plastic stretched over them.

They shifted when she stepped on, and she had to catch herself on Scott's shoulder. She leaned and fumbled the straps.

"Other way," Scott said. He jumped in the snow and fixed the shoes himself. He climbed out and strapped on his own. He turned on his headlamp, then Claire's. Sam handed them poles.

"We ready?" Scott said.

They cut the snow machines' headlamps and instantly the world was three glowing embers. They started out, but almost immediately her shoes caught the powder. She leaned on one foot and worked the other free, but the next step it happened again.

The headlamps swung back at her. "Step higher," Scott said.

"What?"

"Higher. You ever wear your dad's loafers? Walk like that."

It was difficult, but eventually she squared a step, and another, and then it was working, they were fanning up the mountain. As she climbed, Claire peered at the surrounding darkness. For such open wilderness, it felt close around her. She had her radius of light and smoking breath, beneath which passed snow, like seafloor in the lamp of a submarine. Brush appeared, its tangled shadow stalking wide of her, and then cattails, their heads so thick the snow couldn't fall through. She saw birches, invisible in that whiteness except as a picket of shadows.

The creek they followed corralled her Scott's direction. When she reached him, he was inspecting boulders in the current. He stepped to one, then to the opposite bank. He offered a pole and helped her across. With Sam on the first bank, they fanned up the drainage, their headlamps flashing the water.

After a while, Scott called the girl's name. "An–die!" he called. And then Sam joined him, "An–die!" Claire expected an echo, but there was none. The night swallowed it.

"An–die!" Scott said, and then said: "Monitor, where are you? Let's hear it."

"An–die!" she called.

"Louder," he said, and she called out again: "An–die! An–die, where are you, girl?"

They passed through timber, the pines slipping among them. It was hard going, her legs gelatinous and quivery, but she kept on. They came out in a meadow, where the creek vanished in drifts. Her lamp passed through thickets, at the deepest of which she paused and parted branches, craning her beam at the shadows.

"An–die!" Scott called.

"An–die!" Sam echoed.

It was farther, near the top of the meadow, that their voices found one another. "An–die," Sam said, and his tone lay as a platform for Scott, who after a pause sang, "Oh, my sweet An–die!"

They fell silent, peering in brush, but their melody lingered. Finally Scott took it up again. "You're caught in the snow…"

"Don't know where to go…" Sam said.

And after a moment Scott crowned it: "Come out from the woods, and we'll take you home!"

"An–die!" Sam began.

"Oh, my sweet An–die!"

And then together: "Caught in the snow, don't know where to go, come out from the woods and we'll take you home!"

"An–die!" Claire began, and they loved it, they howled: "Oh, my swe–eet An–die!"

"Belt it, Monitor!"

She sang: "Caught in the snow, don't know where to go, come out from the woods and we'll take you home!"

"An–die," Sam began.

They were singing like that, and searching the timber over the meadow, when night paled to morning. They reached the rock field at the top of the basin and circled back to the machines.

In the tent, they flopped on cots and melted together as a single thing, their nerves interwoven. They were so tired, so linked, that it seemed any one of them could touch any other and it would be permissible. It would be no different than touching oneself. Once, Claire walked outside and watched a helicopter thumpet up the mountain, its nose to the pines. As it lowered, the snow beneath it billowed and raced off. But then she went inside again. She wished to dwell in that heat forever.

That afternoon, the search was suspended. Weather had moved in, a blackening howl that surged the tent walls, knocking gear from the shelves and once blowing out the heater. They were joined by others, other heat and voices. Then that evening, the call came through: they were taking people down.

They walked out into blackness and hard cold. Near the tent idled a massive snowcat, the storm whirling its headlamps. They piled in with other guys, guys from County. Finally the engine snorted and they lurched into motion. As they descended, the guy next to Claire wiped his glove on the fogged window. "Not looking good," he said.

When no one replied, he said, "This one's on the books."

They nosed off a ledge and down a steep slope of powder. No one endorsed the man's opinion, but also no one disputed him, and soon the air sagged with defeat. They seemed already to have called it. The group of them, in that cab, seemed already disbanded.

"They won't call it," Claire said.

No one answered.

She said, "Well they haven't called it yet. It's still going."

The village appeared in the windshield, a milky haze from which the hotel and lodge gradually dissociated. The cat parked at the lodge and cut its engines. "We're still doing this," Claire said, but the men were gathering gear, wandering off. She managed to marshal maybe five of them, Scott and Sam included, but only because they were too tired to resist. "Let's go, let's get some rest," she said, herding them towards the hotel. She guided them through the lobby and into the elevator. In her room, they peeled off coats and snow pants and hung them in the bathroom. They draped socks and gloves on every doorknob, rod, lampshade. "Okay, what do we want?" She picked up the phone. "I'll get food. What do we want?"

But when the kid from the kitchen knocked at the door with soup and tuna sandwiches, with French fries, pasta and rolls, no one answered. He knocked again, then swore under his breath and pushed the cart up the hall.

In the room, they'd collapsed like narcoleptics on the bed and floor. Someone had hit the lights, but that was it. They lay where they'd fallen.

Though even sleeping (if she could be said to be sleeping—it was more nearly a fugue of near-sleep not wholly distinct from waking, from trudging drifts)—even then, there was an ache in her. She lay on the bed between two of them, one before and one behind, and at some hour, in the dark, she reached for them. The one before her she gripped with her hands, drawing him near. But he was out cold. She pressed into the body behind her. He didn't respond, but she stayed there, coaxing, until he stirred and they stirred together. It would go on like that, she believed. Garments drawn aside, he would press and discover her. They would fall through shared breath. But no—they were still again. He was sleeping.

In the morning, a shovel was scraping under the window. A newspaper thumped the door. And in the room's pale light, it was hard to believe any part of the night was recoverable.

"Let's go, we've got to go," she said, climbing stiffly from the bed. She shuffled over them, their sleeping forms, and hit the lights. She went to the window, already pulling on gloves. Only nothing had changed. The lodge, maybe sixty feet off, was visible only as a grainy thing, an irregularity of shadow. A man in a neon coat trudged at the wind.

"It snowing?" someone mumbled.

For a long while, as the rest of them slept, she remained at the window. Something would happen, she believed. The weather would lift. But it snowed, and gradually the men in her room rose and shuffled to the bathroom, sorted for coats. They wandered out, thanking her vaguely. Soon, it was just Sam and Scott.

A radio squawked, and Sam punched buttons. "Repeat," he said, resting the receiver against his eyes. There was static, then: "No go. We're shutting it down."

Then the two of them left, too.

That day and the day following, Claire stayed in her room. Something still would happen, she believed. Snow machines would convene at the lodge. But the weather cleared, and rather than snow machines the village filled with smiling throngs. They packed the chairlifts. Under a canopy by the lodge, a woman was giving massages.

After checking out, she stopped by the bar. Luke was wiping counters.

"Well lookie here," he said.

She mounted a stool. "What're you doing?"

"What's it look like?" He walked down the bar and flipped on the TV. "I'm leaving," she said. It hurt to say. It was like the pronouncement of some dreaded thing, past which there was no orientation, no gravity. Only Luke was confused. "Again?" he said. "You've got to make up your mind."

He had no idea about any of it.

"I know."

"That's your problem," he said. "You're always going somewhere."

Outside, every surface was aflame. Eyes throbbing, she made her way to the parking lot, where the valet had her car.

The road off the mountain wound through cabins and condos, then fell through heavy timber. She drove slowly, her breath fogging. It was weeks before the doctor from Spokane, skiing the glades under the lift, glimpsed the mitten or part of the hat, the pink scrap clinging to brush—glimpsed it and skied on. It wasn't her, he decided. What was her name again? Angie something. Annie. He'd read about it. But they'd lost her out of bounds, out in the canyons. You died in the canyons, skiing beyond the ropes. Within, things were managed. You never died within.

CONTRA

ONE AFTERNOON, SEVERAL YEARS after my first indiscretion and maybe two days after my most recent, I came home and saw in the corner the most elaborate, ornate broom. There it leaned, its handle thick, expensive wood, wood like the kind the guy upstate whittles down in the shape of otters. At the top was a leather hoop, at the bottom a thatch of bristles fanned from an elegant braid. A broom. It hadn't been there when I'd left that morning, and so I froze when I saw it, my coat partway down my arms. Then I removed the coat all the way and tossed it at the coatrack. Only the next thing I discovered was the coatrack wasn't there. My coat fell through empty air and landed on a…well, I wasn't sure what it landed on. I lifted the coat and saw beneath it a halved, sanded log set on sturdy pegs. It was a bench, but not a bench I'd seen in my house before, and, like the broom, not a bench from this century. Beside the bench was a rack of antique tools—a scoop, a hook, a brush—hearth tools, though we don't have a hearth. I straightened up and looked around. And you know that painting where you see one Indian in the trees, then boom, see the whole war party? Well, on the wall I saw an analog clock with actual ticking arms and everything. Stacked on the coffee table were old board games, their boxes lettered with faded, psychedelic fonts, the children on the top box freckled and corduroyed. Beside the games was a quilt. A quilt! This was our apartment, I was pretty sure. What was going on?

I was in the kitchen inspecting a fruit basket (was the basket new or just the fruit?) when the back door opened. Now, we have a back door, but our place is a walk-up and to come in from the back you have to climb four flights of stairs. No one had ever used that back door. It was painted shut, I'd thought. But there was Em, freshened from the cold, her bangs plastered to her forehead. In her arms was a load of veggies—carrots, potatoes, et cetera. She dumped them on the table and pushed back her hair. "Well hey!"

We didn't typically buy veggies, and when we did we carried them in a sack, not in our arms. Plus the veggies we bought had stickers on them, and looked hard and firm, like they'd come with a warranty. These things on the table looked like something pulled from a plant. "Hi…" I said. I wasn't sure what to say.

"Work go all right?" She carried the carrots to the sink and started scraping them with a peeler. I wasn't aware we'd owned a peeler.

"What? Oh, yeah," I said.

She glanced back, smiled.

"You?" I said.

"It was good."

"The elevator busted?"

"Is it?"

"You took the stairs."

"Well, I thought I'd use my feet. I have feet, I thought I'd use them. Would you hand me that yam?"

I looked at the table, where there was something that maybe was a yam, but on second thought was a potato. I grabbed something else that could be the yam.

"The other one," she said.

But there still were several candidates for yam.

"This…" she grabbed the yam, and waved it at my nose, "…is a yam. A tuber."

She returned to the sink, where she whipped the thing with her peeler.

It was a while before I spoke. "Em," I said.

"Paul."

To satisfy myself that it all was real, I glanced in the living room at the broom and bench and tools and clock, at the games and quilt. I studied the fruit basket and free-range veggies. "Babe, it seems like you've got something going," I said.

She loaded her arms with skinned yams and carrots and carried them past me to the cutting board.

"Or not," I said.

"See, this is the problem." She chopped the carrots.

"What's the problem?"

She made a hard chop, a carrot nub tumbling from the board, then whipped back her hair and pointed at things with her knife. "See that? Paul, that's food. I'm making food. And in there?" She jabbed her knife at the living room. "That's a quilt."

See but I already knew those things.

Then she said, "Paul, when food and quilts seem strange that's a problem. That's when you've forgotten how it's done."

I shouldn't have asked, but did. "How what's done?"

She'd resumed chopping, but then stopped again and drew a long breath. She watched the knife in her hand.

"Forget it," I said.

"How being a person is done, Paul."

She finished the carrots and yams, then did other things to other foods. She took down a wooden bowl we hadn't owned twenty-four hours earlier and shook in flour, seeds. Soon pans simmered, timers beeped. After a while, we ate what actually was a pretty good meal, though it was light on salt.

She'd worked it out of her system, I decided. That happened sometimes, where she got stuff in her system. I loved her anyways. Only later, coming up the hall to the bedroom, I found her standing at the door.

It's never good when your beloved stands firmly in a doorway. "Em," I said.

"Paul."

I stepped forward, but a hand met my chest. I looked at the hand and had nothing to say.

She looked past me then, and nodded at the guest room, where, following her gaze, I discovered the bed was turned down, and the lamp on. "Whoa, whoa," I said.

"Paul, listen."

"You want me to sleep in there?"

"Paul." Her palm hadn't left my chest. "How we did things before? That's not how we're doing them now."

"You want me to sleep in the guestroom?"

"I want you..." she smoothed my shirt and dropped her hand, "...I want *both* of us, doing things how they're done."

"You want me sleeping across the hall?"

"For now."

"Well, fuck me."

"Paul..."

"Can I get my pajamas?"

"Paul, listen. This is part of it. How you feel right now? Your..." she wiggled her fingers at my lower parts, "...urges? Men have had those urges. Okay, since the dawn of time, your brothers have felt what you're feeling."

"Dawn of time?"

"But there's a way you do things. There's always been a way."

For all my years of indiscretions, it was only then I suspected Em knew something. The broom, the food, now this—it was all vaguely punitive.

"Look," she said. "Ask me out."

"What?"

"That's how this starts. Ask me out."

"Now?"

"Here I am."

I thought if I stood there this would blow over. When it didn't, I drew a breath. "Em, will you go out with me?"

I felt ridiculous saying that. But as if flattered, as if the idea surprised and thrilled her, Em's features lifted. "Paul Meyers, yes. I'd love to go out with you."

That was the ticket. I put my hand on her side and moved my mouth to her neck. But a palm met my chest.

"Okay, okay, I just thought…" I said.

"Tomorrow. And remember, we're doing it right."

"Tomorrow," I said.

She shut the door.

Had she come at me a week earlier with this broom and yam bonanza, this ambush of traditional practices, I wouldn't have gone for it. A broom? I don't think so. Luiza came Tuesdays and brought brooms of her own. Hearth tools? What were we, the Ingalls Wilders? At the end of the night, when she turned me back from the room, I'd have tried just once to change her mind. Then I'd have hit the town.

But that week, as it happened, was the week of Grace Lomeli. Grace was Em's friend from work, one of her best friends. I was drunk, I had her number—let's not get into it. Suffice to say, you can do a thing for years, and feel fine about it, then do it once with real coldness and realize the monster you are. The self-disgust you ought to have felt all along arrives at once, and you drown in it. So Em had a new way of seeing things, a novel approach? I'd try that. Certainly I had more to lose by not trying it.

The night after my dismissal from the bedroom, I showered and shaved and slapped on fragrant balm, dressed in pressed slacks. I didn't know what I was doing. For all my dalliances, I hadn't in my life gone on a proper date. Still, I touched my hair in the mirror, and studied one cheek and the other. There was a way it was done, I knew that. I'd seen old shows. He opens doors, pulls out chairs. I could do that. I blew a kiss at the mirror and went up the hall. I knocked at what since yesterday had been Em's room.

A hairdryer was running. I knocked again. "Hello?"

"Not like this!" she called back.

"What?"

"The front door!"

I looked down the hall.

"I'll be right out!" she said.

I walked down the hall and out the door, and after a minute knocked at the door. I knocked again. When she did answer, it was in a dark dress and high boots, a gray shawl on her shoulders. She was stunning, her hair molded but careless, so that she gazed at me from under a lock of it. "Jesus," I said.

"Hello, Mr. Meyers."

"Em, look at you."

"Look at you!"

Until then, I'd not anticipated our date. It was a chore I'd agreed to. But seeing her in the doorway, I wanted to take her wherever she'd let me. "All right, let's go. Let's do it," I said, and started down the hall.

When she didn't follow, I came back to the door. "What?"

She looked at me funny.

"Should we take the stairs?"

"Paul…" she said.

"What?"

She dimmed an eye. "Well, it's a date, Paul."

"A date, I know. Let's go."

"Well, but it's a date. Shouldn't you bring something?"

"Bring…?"

"I don't know, a gift. Flowers."

I looked at my hands, as if flowers might materialize.

"You should have flowers," she said.

"I'll get some."

"Wonderful. Okay."

"I'll be back." I started down the hall.

"Only…"

I came back. "What is it?"

She thought about something. "Only not tonight," she said.

"What do you mean?"

"Tonight's off, I think."

"*Off?*"

"Isn't that what'd happen? He knocks at the door, she's underwhelmed?"

"You're *underwhelmed?*"

"I think we're off for tonight, Paul. That's all right. Tomorrow. Just say you want another chance."

She was waiting.

"You want me to say that?"

"Let's hear it."

I said what she wanted.

And she nodded. "Sure. You're a nice young man making an honest effort. I respect that. Tomorrow night then, seven o'clock." She walked back in the apartment. "Tell you what, I'm pooped. I'm hitting the hay. You need your pajamas?"

My second attempt was no good either, though I made it as far as the restaurant before she pulled the plug (I'd checked my phone). The third attempt, she caught me gazing past her at the TV in the bar. I actually was watching the woman under the TV, but that wasn't the kind of information I could fight back with. Em was up and moving for the door. I followed.

It was the following night I figured it out. Em had gone to bed and I'd retired to the guestroom, where I lay on the twin mattress, watching the ceiling. What happened was I suddenly had a view of myself, lying there with my feet hanging off the bed, snug in my PJs, like a fool. And I couldn't take it. I was an adult man with adult needs and dignity. Before I could calm myself I'd leapt from the bed and burst into the hall. I pounded Em's door. "Emily!" It was midnight or so.

I pounded again. "Em!"

She cracked the door.

"Let me in there."

"Go to bed."

"I'm sick of this."

She tried to shut the door, but I jammed my foot in the doorway. "I'm coming in that room. That's where I sleep."

"No, you aren't."

"Yes, and we're fucking. End of story."

"Paul…"

"That's what's happening, Em."

"You're going to bed. We've got our date tomorrow."

There we stood, the door dividing us. "Our date," I said.

"We've talked about this."

"Our date."

"Paul…"

I took my foot from the door, and moved up the hall hitting light switches.

"What're you doing?" she said.

"Let's have a date. That's good."

"Paul."

"Get your coat. No time like the present."

I didn't mean it, of course. I just was blowing off steam. But when I'd lighted the whole apartment and come back up the hall, there she was in her coat. I stood before her like an idiot.

"Well?" she said.

"Really?"

"Are we going?"

"Yeah." I looked around. "Okay."

It wasn't much for romance, that first date. We went for coffee, then walked through the park, the wind billowing our pajamas. We found an ice cream shop, and once inside just studied the bins. It was too cold for ice cream. But what I learned that night was it was okay. I needn't know anything, or get anything right. I just had to press. The rest was her business.

We got home that night and I grabbed her from behind. She squirmed free, but I got her again. She squirmed free a second time, and whirled like a badger. "Go," she said, pointing. "Your room. Now."

And I did, I went to my room. I strolled up the hall. But really I didn't do anything. I just was me, and let her corral me.

That powered us along. I advanced, and before my advances Em erected walls, or sails, rather, that filled with my advances and propelled our dates. We went to restaurants, movies. We visited flea markets, an old-timey mill. Em was happy, I think. We were acting how she wanted. Where a ship can sail except where the wind pushes it, I'm not sure. But we hadn't thought of that. We were having fun.

The date I remember best was a night of ice skating in the park. Now, I'm a talented skater. Let's get that clear from the get-go. But whereas until that night my talent had been just talent, had been cool but useless, like an heirloom coin, it in the confines of a date was the strength I used to press the date and break it open. In other words, it was perfect. Out I skimmed on the ice, one long coast and the next, hands at my back. I glided, right skate and left, left and right, my rhythms an expression of nature. All of it, each exquisite detail, eroded Em's barriers. For her own part, she was like a clumsy foal, chipping along with her arms waving around. But that was perfect. The disparity of our talents was like a lever to be leaned on. I passed her skating backwards. I lifted a skate, stretching my quad.

"Oh, fuck you," she said, thrashing her arms like a cartoon dupe at the edge of a cliff.

"Now, now," I said, swiveling along.

"How do you do it?"

"Skate? You have to find that inner strength..." I pushed backwards and went again on one skate, lowering in a kind of reverse airplane.

"Well, that's nice."

"It is nice."

"Show me," she said.

"I don't know." I was up again, gliding a long arc. I

disappeared on her left, then reappeared on her right, still skating backwards. Have I mentioned I can skate?

"What don't you know?" she said.

"I should respect your boundaries."

"Oh, here we go."

"Skating's intimate."

"His big opportunity," she said.

"Well, think it over." With a neat little hop I was skating forward, gliding left and right, skimming off through the chill. I flew through a lap and returned to her. "Well?" I said.

"You can teach me. Teaching's different."

"Oh?"

"Teachers touch you."

Em had attended Catholic schools. I wanted to say something about teachers touching her, something pure gold, but starting over as we had, she had become a guarded thing, a mystery, and damned if I'd wreck the mood with a gag about pervert priests.

"You want me to touch you?" I said.

"I want you to teach me."

At first, it just was hands. I drew her along by her mittens, steadying her balance. When that was insufficient, I skated closer and touched her sides, a leg of mine between hers. Then I glided around and moved with her from behind, my hips guiding the pair of us. It was extraordinary, those moments on the ice. The full surface of her was possibility, and my every nerve, neck to knee, pressed that possibility's frontier.

She watched her skates mostly, but at one point she lifted her face and gazed with me at the edge of the pond, at the dark park beyond, the city lights. Our breath mingled. "You like this?" she said.

"I do," I said, and I did.

That night on the sofa, with the broom watching, we (and I don't know how else to say this) necked. That sounds childish, and it was, but also it was fierce and erotic and I remember being not at all displeased with such action on a sixth date. When things got too heavy, Em scampered off to the bedroom. I wandered to the guestroom. But I felt good that night. It was as if I'd arrived, and yet was still arriving, if that makes sense.

Where it culminated, our dabbling in old values, was a night maybe a month later, when after pasta and too much wine, we went home and dropped our coats on the bench, and flung the quilt from the sofa. We'd planned only to neck, but immediately tore off our clothes, and were pressing at flesh, biting. We fucked mindlessly, like dimwitted animals. I remember grabbing at her, at her breasts, pulling her breasts, gripping her mouth, swept along in savagery I'd not known till then was in me. She thrashed back, so that it was a kind of combat from which I emerged victorious only by pinning her down, by pressing her face in the cushions. Bar none, it was the fullest sex of my life, my every fiber an instrument of penetration. Afterwards, we laughed and laughed.

Though maybe where the experiment really ended was a week or so later, when after a long day at work and an insignificant meal (the both of us too tired to cook), we fucked like it was nothing, like who cared. Sex, after brushing and flossing, might've been the third habit recommended by dentists. Afterwards, she prepped for work. I dicked around on my phone.

I might as well admit it. My unfortunate night with Grace Lomeli, who probably was Em's best friend, was in fact two unfortunate nights, the second coming that spring, in May or so. I don't remember what happened. I was out with friends. Then I was home with Grace, at her home. We were in bed. She'd been texting me, I remember that. I'm sure it was one of those here's-an-opportunity things. There were reasons not to pursue that opportunity, but apparently not sturdy reasons. There I was.

When it was over, we lay in the dark. I'd not wanted to be there to begin with, and so was ready to dress and go home, but before I could move Grace propped on an elbow and looked me over. A long while she looked at me, waiting I suppose for some reciprocal gaze, but that wasn't happening. Finally she drew a breath. "Paul, what the fuck?"

It was the question floating in my own head.

"Why are you even here?"

"Grace…"

She threw back the covers and swung her legs out. She passed in front of the bed.

"Grace…" I said, but she cut me off. "No, I'm serious. You tell me, Paul."

"I like you," I said, and it must've sounded as irrelevant as it was. She laughed.

"I do," I said.

"Well, that's incredible. That's heartwarming."

"Can I not like you?"

"Paul, people like hamburgers. Okay Skittles, they like Skittles. Would you come here and fuck Skittles? What're you doing here?"

"I don't know," I said.

She lifted a hand, and dropped it. "He doesn't know."

"I'm sorry."

"I'll ask Em. We'll see what she thinks."

I was out of bed then, pulling up my jeans. Grace watched me. "I don't know what to tell you," I said.

"You're here, though, aren't you? Did you think of that?"

"Where's my shirt?"

"You're here. You come here. Good luck denying that."

Grace didn't follow through on her threat. Like most of us, she prefers secret knowledge to confrontation. Still, there must've been something in how she acted, or how I acted—there must've been something. Em knew, I'm pretty sure. It was two days later I came home from work and it was gone—the TV, the microwave, all of it. The kitchen table was heaped with veggies. I hadn't removed my coat before she made it clear. "We're doing it this time. I mean it," she said.

I dropped my keys on the table. "All right."

"Nothing half-assed."

I was reluctant to ask, but asked anyway. "Something happen?"

She had the broom in hand and was working it like an electrified wand, like she couldn't let go. "No," she said. "Nothing special. More of the same."

I thought about that, then peeled off my coat. "Can I help?"

It was then she dropped the broom and went to the refrigerator (still there, thankfully). She snatched something from under a magnet.

"What's this?"

"It's how you can help."

"What is it?"

She pushed it in my hands. "Read."

The paper was a flier trimmed with colorful, grandstand bunting. At the top, in a font I associate with Wanted posters, was a single, emphatic announcement: CONTRA!

"It's something people do." She took the flier and stuck it back on the fridge.

"What people?"

She'd returned to the broom. "People who want to get laid again," she said.

The Peabody Grange was out of town, up in the county where bearded artisans whittled their critters. Em drove, the city's headache of blared horns loosening to a five-lane blast path of RV dealerships and malls, and King China Buffets, out of which tapered a narrow state highway, alone in the hills. From the beginning, it was her show. Hands at ten and two, her gaze locked on the windshield. On her features was the sternness of a woman rushing a loved one to the emergency room, which may not have been far from her actual mentality, though it was a different kind of room (what's a grange, anyhow?), and a different kind of emergency.

And me? What was my mentality? Well, I wouldn't have

driven 50 miles to clop heels with folksy strangers without her demanding it. That's fair to say. Still, some part of me was glad to be in that car. There was something, I don't know. That second night with Grace. You ever do a thing and think, God what a dipshit move, why'd I do that? That's so unlike me. Then do it again and think, Wait, *is* this unlike me? It maybe went deeper than sleazing around, is what I'm saying. What if on some marrowish level I in fact was a sleaze, and stood no better chance of stopping than emus stand of flying? Had I thought of that? And I don't know, it scared me. Fucking up's one thing, but who wants to be a fuck-up? So it was okay, being in that car. Contra dancing sounded dull, but at the wheel was a woman absolutely convinced she could fix me, and I needed that.

We arrived at a dusty lot of pickups and hillbilly beaters (though also more Acuras than you'd think), at the rear of which stood what looked like a church. Crossing the lot, Em hooked her arm in mine. "Paul, get that look off your face." I hadn't had any look on my face, though that probably was the look she referred to, that expression of blank, checked-out boredom. Only I wasn't bored. I'd have gone anywhere she led me, have tried anything.

Inside (the Peabody Grange really is a church, with a coatroom in what once had been a vestibule, a stage built on the altar, and, believe it or not, Coke machines stuffed in the confessionals), we found maybe thirty strangers watching the band tune fiddles. Em took it in, surveying the room as she might survey aisles in a store where she hadn't shopped, then turned and set a palm on my chest. "Paul," she said.

"I know."

"We're doing this."

"I know, Em."

"Listen. All the way. Don't..." She was frustrated.

"What?"

"This needs to be us today. We need to be this."

I was ready to be this, that, I'd have been anything she

wanted, so long as it wasn't what I was already, or feared I was, which was a sex emu.

"Paul," she said.

"You need to show me what we're doing."

"I know, but you need to do it."

"Show me."

She glanced at the room, then gripped my hand and led us through the crowd. We would talk to these strangers, it seemed like. I didn't like that, but whatever. My job at the moment wasn't liking things, it was going where herded, just as the job of a mouse cupped under a jar, or maybe a rat, is going where the jar bumps it. We approached some geezers drinking coffee. Greeting the first one, Em laid a hand on his spotted wrist. That exceeded a threshold of intimacy I don't like exceeding with strangers (unless you count the times I exceed that and other thresholds quite readily), but so went jar, so went rat, and so when Em stepped back and introduced me, I grabbed the bastard myself. "Paul Meyers, pleasure to meet you," I said, working his arm like a gear shifter. I grabbed the geezer next to him. "Paul Meyers," I said. It was awkward, but hey.

And when the dance started, I decided I'd keep it going. I knew nothing, but that didn't matter. I'd go where the room pushed me. By way of preliminaries, the caller trotted us in a circle, left and right. He contracted the circle, then dilated it, the more veteran dancers beginning then to yelp and nod and embellish their steps with little clippety-clop skips. Hey, and where it went I went. Whatever. It wasn't just the caller, either. In a ring like that everyone sees you, and you'd be surprised how well that holds you in place. It gets you moving, and once moving any deviation you make from the steps or tempo, you feel the room's pressure and get back in line. The short of it was I danced. I went, *and back and two and round to the left and turn and two and back to the right, now up and two and step to the front and back and two and back to the start,* without exerting any will, without thinking, nothing.

We paired off, and do-si-doed and swung. I didn't know do-si-do or swing either, of course, but if there's a force more commanding than the eyes of thirty strangers, it's the eyes of your Emily. There she was, whirling in my arms with her hair flying sideways, or else stamping boots, jutting her elbows. She was so happy, dancing as humans always have danced, the people around her people and simply so. And seeing her happy, it was easy, it was automatic. I stamped my own feet, jutted my own elbows. I clapped, clapped. It was like a membrane, her happiness. I needed not to break it, and so when the membrane stretched, when I missed a step or danced too slow, when my clapping grew halfhearted, I felt the stretching and eased it, got back in line.

"Having fun?" she shouted.

"Yeah!"

"Don't lie!"

"I am!" I yelled.

And I was. Contra wasn't fun—it wasn't that. But the effect was good, things were right. Plus, it turns out, I kind of know what I'm doing. I'm kind of a contrasseur.

"Look at you!" Em said.

I'd stamped my foot, then let the beat stretch and stamped again. I clapped, yipped.

"A natural!" she cried.

We were in groups of four, the music sawing and warbling, our hands linked, trotting clockwise and counter. For a New England tradition, contra sure does resemble witchcraft, which, remember, is not a beloved New England tradition. We backed up for Em's do-si-do with her stranger, my do-si-do with mine. We swung our strangers, then made swim moves to others. Lo and behold the next hand I grasped was Em's. Her happiness was radiant, flying around that floor, and to contra well I needed only to center myself in that radiance, and not chance its margins.

"You're so good!" she shouted.

"You think?"

"You're a natural," she said again.

And maybe I am, who knows. We did dance the whole contra, every song, then go home and in the morning wake up. The days, like some contra all their own, have stretched a line through weeks, the weeks through months, and indeed I've done it. So far, at least, the guy Em hopes to see when she looks at me is the guy I've been.

Only I must say, I must say. There was a moment, that day at the grange that became late day, the sun flat in the rafters, and then became evening, Em and I whirling, swinging, the both of us streaming sweat—there was a moment that night when, moving up the line, I found in my arms a woman who wasn't Em. I thought she was Em, but then looked and she wasn't. The stranger herself seemed surprised, as if she'd expected another man. Only I wasn't that guy, she wasn't Em, and have you ever had that moment, that brush with a stranger you know absolutely is the start of something? Well, for eight counts this woman spun in my arms, her back hot on my palm, her breath on my neck, the room beyond us an irrelevant blur...

Then of course she was gone (this was barn dancing, remember). But can you picture a contra? Is that a silly question? Go watch a contra. If you can, stand back and view the thing. Because there they are, those neat pairs handed down through the ages. And there they are now, whirling apart, whirling apart. The dance corrects them. It presses them into couples. But then again they're whirling, again parting, pressing off through the room. So that you wonder about a thing like that, an old thing, a form. It holds you, no doubt. Everyone knows it holds you. Only you wonder what older things it someday fails to hold back.

AN INCH OFF THE GROUND

SINCE HER DAD'S DIAGNOSIS (nothing serious—they'll pluck his prostate like popping a cork and he'll be back to hang gliding and cycling) my wife's been in overdrive. She's baked casseroles, thrown pillows wherever he might sit, bought him a cushy toilet seat. When she's not at his side, she's wringing her hands. Also, it's made her interested in my dad, a topic we've avoided.

The other night, we were eating one of the surplus casseroles. "Tell me about him," she said.

"Dad?"

"You never talk about him."

She knew why I didn't talk about him. My dad wasn't a dad. When I was two, he'd moved to a duplex and drunk till he died. I didn't resent it, at least I didn't anymore. But there wasn't much to say.

"Tell me about him. I want a story," she said.

"A story?"

"I know he wasn't...I know. But there should be something good."

"Good?"

"You don't have a single good story?"

Besides the times he fell down or ran into shit, there wasn't much to tell. But I did have one story. "Okay," I said.

"You got one? Hold on." She got some wine, and came back and sat down.

—

I didn't live with my dad, as I've said. My mom and I lived across town. I never would've seen him, not for a minute, had Mom wanted it that way. He was desiccated, incapable of focus, of speech. Any legal proceeding would've nipped him from our lives as neat as the prostate from my father-in-law's ass. But Mom loved Dad. They'd been drunks together. Quitting, she said, had been like leaving him in a burning house. So instead of shunning him, she sent me over now and again with food and flowers. This was once I was old enough to drive, and old enough, if needed, to defend myself. Not that that would've been necessary. In the years I knew Dad, which were few (he died when I was seventeen), I never once saw him intend harm, or be capable of it. He just lay in his chair.

The story I had for Kate was one of the times I visited him. It was a Saturday. My mom gave me the flowers and trays of food, like we were catering a funeral, which we kind of were. I took Trent Avenue past the rail yards and warehouses. Dad's building, as I've said, was a duplex, the division of which extended to the curb. On one side was his neighbor's lawn, on the other side his weeds. His gate had been ajar since they'd started growing, and now was woven ajar. Even off its hinges, it would've stood straight up. I always imagined him on the day he'd moved in, his arms full of every bottle he'd drink in fifteen years, kicking the gate open and going inside, and that being the last sunlight he saw.

The day of my story, I remember, was hot. Grasshoppers popped from the weeds. Of course, inside, things were awful. Pizza boxes littered the floor. Newspapers accumulated in corners, as if blown there by wind. One of the things I did on my visits was clean. What else would I do? I'd walk through the rooms, collecting trash and sweeping, while he lay in his chair. From other rooms, or from the basement, I'd ask questions at a conversational volume. He couldn't hear, but he couldn't have heard had I straddled the chair and shouted in his face.

"Dad?" I said, and didn't listen for a reply. The TV was going. I walked in the kitchen and swept trash from the counter so I could put down the sandwiches and daisies. He was in the living room, on his chair, the canned laughter wafting from his set. What did he look like, sprawled there with his open mouth? He was like a man on a ventilator, except there was no man, just a rickety ventilator.

I hated my dad. I didn't know him, but hated him, or was embarrassed, which at sixteen is fiercer than hatred. Why'd he do this? He lacked restraint, was how my mom put it, but I didn't see how restraint figured in. When you wanted something, and couldn't hold back—that was lacking restraint. Dad was a sack of shit. Did he want that? I doubted it. Booze had taken him over was all. He'd been a coward.

I felt no obligation to him, is the point. I'd only gone there for Mom, whose life was hard enough without a kid dragging heels. For Mom, and because it was cover. That maybe was the one thing Dad was good for. I could be there, but really be elsewhere. What, would he tell? What would the drooling fuck have to say that people would listen to, if he could speak to begin with, if he even knew when another person was in the room? Lightning fast, I tore through the house bagging garbage, or stuffing it from sight. I wiped counters, windowsills, jammed the flowers in a Popov quart. I texted mom: DAD AWAKE. GONNA STAY. BACK 2MORROW, and was out of there. "See ya, pop!" I called from the door. "You're looking sharp!"

This'd happened frequently, more times than it hadn't. I drove to Trev's house, which wasn't far, and woke him up. We got forties. You're thinking that's ironic, and it is, and I knew that. But this was different. Trev and I liked drinking. We knew we shouldn't (his dad had problems, too), but it was fun. I guess we lacked restraint.

Where the day became different, and became a story I'd tell my wife, was when Hanratty called. Some kid he knew was throwing a party.

"Who?" Trev said. We had the phone on speaker.

"Some kid. Got his dad's place."

"Choice," Trev said.

"His dad out of town?" I asked.

"Oh, big time."

"Yeah?"

"Dude's dead."

"Whoa," Trev said, "whoa."

"Got his dad's place for real. Fucking *got* it."

"He's having a party?"

"People grieve different ways, man. We're all different snowflakes."

"Long as he doesn't care."

"This kid? He doesn't care."

Trev was too drunk to drive, and since I was too drunk, too, we both drove, to make it fair. The kid's house was out of town, on a lake. He was rich, I guessed, or his dad had been rich, and now he was. I followed Trev up the highway. It was late by then, the sun in the pines. I called my mom.

"Where are you?" she said.

"At Dad's."

"Why's it sound like a car?"

"I'm getting him dinner."

Mom's gone too, now, so I can't ask, but my impression is parenting for her was an intricate accommodation. She had to know I wasn't at Dad's (what, would I sleep on pizza boxes?), but also she had to know I shouldn't have been at Dad's. I should've been, as I was, with friends. But also she must've known I drank with my friends, and must've worried my escape from Dad would prove an avenue to him, so to speak. There's a poem I read once, about a tent pole with slack tethers, unless the wind blows and tightens them. My mom's not the pole, as I think of her, but she's in the tent with hands at the pole, listening for wind.

"Well, be careful. Be sure he eats," she said.

This still isn't a story I'd have told Kate. Excepting certain particulars of weather, this could've been any Saturday from 1997 to 1999. I might as well describe brushing my teeth. No, where it became different was at the party. This was on Loon Lake, I think, one of those lakes north of town. As promised, it was a banger. Kids were everywhere, good and hammered. Music blared. A girl I knew came swimming with me, then ran off. I was walking up the dock in my birthday suit when Hanratty appeared and introduced me to the kid. "Yo," he said. "This is Sean."

I couldn't see him. The house lights were at his back. "Hey," I said.

"The kid whose house it is," Ratty explained.

"Oh, shit." I stood straighter, my pecker hanging there, and shook the kid's hand. "How do you do?"

He nodded up the dock. "Get a swim?"

"Yeah."

"Well, good. Mi casa, su casa."

And it started there. "Es actually his papa's casa. La casa de la his padre," Hanratty said. Then, putting a hand at his mouth as if to tell a secret, but still speaking at full volume, he said, "Es muerto, by the way. His papa's muerto."

Hanratty was drunk, but I didn't think that was something you could say, drunk or otherwise. I stood there, unsure what to do. But the kid laughed.

"Is he not?" Ratty said.

Sean shrugged. "Es veridad."

"Verydad? Verydead?"

They howled and howled. Finally Ratty hit my arm. "Hey, it's cool. He's over it."

"I'm over it," the kid assured me. Then he said, "Hey, your dick's showing. Let's get a drink."

Inside, I dressed and got a forty. Trev had his forty. We linked arms and drank like newlyweds. But it wasn't long before I drifted over to Sean. Everyone was drifting to Sean. We had to see about this kid. He was in the kitchen, slamming Mickey's and laughing. His dad was dead, yet there he was.

At one point, when things were quiet, I said, "Hey, sorry about…you know."

Others murmured agreement. It was big shit, losing a dad. And Sean acknowledged the sentiment. He took a pull of Mickey's, and, swallowing, patted my shoulder. "Hey, but it's fine, you know?" he said.

"Yeah?"

There maybe were six of us, listening like students. Sean said, "Everyone dies. It happens. But you move on. I'm still breathing."

I remember that floored me, and not just the words but his ease in saying them. I didn't know about death, except that it was a big deal, just as dads were a big deal. When one met the other, it had to be huge. Even for me, who hated his dad, that would've been huge. Yet there was Sean, calm and free. The world, I'd thought, was a certain way. Yet he was above it.

"You know what helps?" he said.

"What?"

"Joking about it. Setting it free."

"Yeah?" Had the kid led an army, I'd have drawn my sword and died for him.

"It was a car wreck, that's how he went. So what do we do?"

"What?" I said.

"Ratty?"

But Ratty already was pouring the car bombs.

Where Sean was, I wanted to be. It was that simple. He floated like a balloon towards some exempt air, and I caught his tether and floated with him. After the first bombs, we did more, then more. Then Sean poured a shot and drove it down the counter, swerving it into the toaster. "Boosh!" he cried, and splashed the shot on the ceiling. It was like the story Mom told about the night she met my dad. It was at a bar, of course. He was alive, she said, electric. He floated an inch off the ground. Sean was like that.

"You're the man," I told him.

He shrugged. "What can I say?"

I was drunk, but the booze was indistinguishable from my discovery of a hero, which I guess is the point here. I said, "Sean, you've got to show me the way."

"The way?"

"I want to be you."

"With hard work," he assured me.

"No, I'm serious. My dad…" I shook my head.

"He croak?"

"Not really. But I mean he doesn't…" I wanted to describe Dad, and his drooling in the chair, his worthlessness, but Sean, just in seeing how I felt, or *that* I felt, had seen enough. "Hey." He put a forty in my hands. "Who cares?"

"That's right."

"Fuck your dad," he said.

"Fuck my dad, yeah. Fuck your dad. Fuck dads."

"Does it matter?" he said.

"Absolutely not."

"Everyone?" Sean shouted. He shouted again, "Excuse me, people?"

Someone softened the music. Sean stood on a chair. "Me and this guy." He looked at me as if to remember my name, then just patted my shoulder. "Me and homeboy, we've got an announcement. From this hour forth, until eternity, dads are fucked. Is that clear? If you have a dad, he's fucked now. I don't know what to tell you. If you like, you can suck a dick. You can suck my dick. Or homeboy's."

No one said anything. People were confused. For my money, however, it was as magnificent a speech as there'd ever been. In school, we'd been reading Gettysburg, Kennedy's Inaugural, I Have a Dream. This was up there. I applauded, pig-whistled. My dad, back at his duplex, could kill himself to the moon. I'd found something above it. "Here, here!" I shouted.

That no one admired the speech, that in fact it was

embarrassing, and rather than applaud people were wincing and smoothing eyebrows—none of that occurred to me. I couldn't let it. For my own purposes, it was too important that the speech be wisdom.

Sean stepped off the chair and gathered people for a drinking game. He said the game was: if your dad was fucked, you drank. No one spoke. He went down the line, poking chests. "Drink, drink, drink…"

Hanratty, poking his own chest, turned up his forty.

Eventually Trev got me aside. "Hey man, are you…?"

I poked his chest. "Drink."

"You okay?"

"I'm over it, dude."

"*Over* it?"

"It's your dad that's fucked."

I don't remember what happened, really. Trev went home. Ratty passed out. Sean and I left, eventually, and carried our drinks down the road, paying house calls. It was a starry night, but the stars blurred and leaked through the trees. At each door, we knocked and put our hands at our backs, something like missionaries, except we held forties. People answered in robes and crazy hair. "Excuse me, ma'am," we'd say, or, "Excuse me, sir. We apologize, but this is a public service announcement. Have you checked your father? There's reports of fucked fathers in the area."

Not a single person said a word. They squinted at us like we were apparitions.

"I'm not sure you understand. Fathers are getting fucked here," Sean explained.

We weren't gone long, I don't think, but when we came back the party was dead. People lay on the floor, on sofas. We kept going. Sean got a marker and wrote DAD FUCKERS POLICE on our shirts. We moved through the house, shaking shoulders. Where people awoke, we knelt and inquired about dads. Sean, nodding thoughtfully, jotted notes. As you'd expect, we only could take it so far. Eventually we lay on chairs and watched TV. Though even then, we didn't concede. Never once did we look at each other and laugh, and marvel at our own stupidity. We were utterly, utterly serious. I remember sitting on that chair, staring at a point between my nose and the TV, believing if I kept my eyes there, right there, the world I needed would be the world I had.

Kate lowered her glass. "What?"

"I know," I said.

"That's your story?"

It'd taken maybe twenty minutes to tell, and I'd not explained it any better than I have now.

"So what, you were drunk? I don't get it."

I told her the rest, how I couldn't sleep and so had driven around. Then had gone to Dad's. I said how I saw him there, the TV light on his face, and for the first time knew what had brought him there, what need in his heart, and not only knew it, but knew I had it, too.

"Okay," she said.

He was asleep. Sometimes you couldn't tell, but he definitely was sleeping. I took his shoes off, and put a blanket on him. I thought about it, then smoothed his hair. It's the one time I remember touching him.

Kate said, "You knew you'd lose him."

I was confused. "Lose?"

"Your dad. He wouldn't always be around."

I love my wife. But if your dad's alive, and always has been, I guess death's the thing. He's alive, alive, alive. What but death could follow? She wouldn't get how a dad could be dead to begin with, dead and gone, until the night you found a pulse.

LIKE GLOVES OF AIR

ALL HIS LIFE HE'D LOVED HIKING, and so he woke that morning and filled a water bottle, cinched his boots. Before leaving, he kissed his sleeping wife, who was off to her mother's later.

"Mm," she said.

"Have a safe trip."

"Mm," she said again.

He watched her in the pillows and sheets, then patted her leg and was off.

The road to the trailhead was a puddled track of switchbacks from which the mountain dropped steeply, as if shorn with a blade. It was dangerous, but the road was the only place he imagined driving, the ditch on the left and cliff on the right not even occurring to him. He might as well have been driving Country Club Lane. Parked and out of the car, he strolled through the forest. He passed through hemlock and spruce, then descended through beds of ferns, the morning cool and smoky. The silence was a blanket pricked with birdcalls and insect chitter. Finally the canopy thinned, and filled with gray, coastal light. What had been ferns became scrubgrass, crowns of rock. Beneath him, stretched to a horizon not easily distinguished from sky, lay the sea. It was an unbroken piece, until he reached the bluff and saw far below the hushed crash of surf. A wind had kicked up.

He followed the bluff trail. Maybe twenty times in his life he'd walked those bluffs, enjoying the terrain, the air. He liked the briny smell and the muted light, liked equally the stiff wind and his coat's protection from it. What a morning. No detail was distinct from the good feeling he had about it. Only that day something changed for John, or changed in him. Or nothing changed, and his eyes simply opened. He'd never know. But walking the bluff, he started to feel something. It was past his shoe, a tickle or whisper. He kept walking, but kept feeling it. Finally he stopped, and stared at where the ground fell away.

He was fine, but then backed into the grass, the cliff suddenly a vague zone over which gravity might swipe a hand and grab him. He stumbled, then caught himself and sat on a rock. That felt safer, sitting down, but then quite independent of himself he kicked at some gravel and watched it spill off the ledge, the noise of its scattering swallowed as wholly as the stones themselves. He didn't know why he'd done that. His heel had simply shot forth, as if before him were this awful thing into which he'd never enter, not ever, but could enter easily enough, should he choose. Had he kicked it away from him? Or, as with entering a pool, had he dipped in a toe…

He sat a long time, breathing heavily. Then he glanced at his water bottle and cast that over the edge. Of course it made no sound, was simply gone. "Jesus," he said. He was shaking, his breath catching. He tried to stand and stumbled again, then stood and made his way through the forest, the whole while stepping carefully, his hands ready at any moment to grasp something, a branch or clump of ferns, anything, as if no cliff need be near for him suddenly to leap from one.

The drive home was terrible. It would take only a jerk of the arm, and on curves take less than that. He'd simply release the wheel. The tires would straighten, the car sail into emptiness. He made it to town, but in town it was worse. At any moment he'd rip the wheel left and obliterate a family on its way to grandma's, or rip it right and clip a teenager chewing gum on the sidewalk. Home, finally, he sat on the sofa and breathed. He was safe at home, the curtains blank and gray. Still, he wondered if he might stand and in that standing join a chain of action leading to the kitchen, where there were appliances and knives. Then he wondered if the sitting itself weren't already involved in that chain, if he weren't already bound to it.

He eased back on the sofa. Okay, he thought, okay. It was his living room. How many Saturdays had he sat in that room and been fine? That's what he was doing, right? He was sitting. Was that dangerous? He breathed again, one long draw of air. Yes. There he was. It was harmless, plain. Sitting in a room. That was all.

He pushed to his feet. That was harmless, too. He inclined his torso, placed his palms on his knees, pushed upright. Okay, he thought. Now we're talking. Standing in a room. He even laughed at himself then, his reflection in the darkened TV something brutish and simian. "Standing in my house," he said aloud.

In the kitchen, he took a glass from the cupboard and poured water. He gazed at the window. What was that? he wondered. Had that been an episode? He'd never had episodes but knew about them. Maybe he'd had an episode. Steve, his friend, had them. He'd have to ask Steve.

His phone buzzed. He picked it up. "Hey."

It was Becky. She'd made it to her mom's. "How was it?" she said.

"How was...?"

"You didn't go?"

"Oh. It was foggy."

"It's the ocean," she said.

"Yeah."

She said something to her mom, and her mom said something back. She added something, then was back with him. "Sorry," she said.

"It's okay."

"So what now, what're you up to?"

"I'm in the kitchen."

"I had something to ask you. I can't remember it."

"What was it?"

"I can't remember. Hold on."

Again she left the phone. He sipped his water, watching a light mist freckle the window. What had happened that morning was over, but he thought he should tell her. Or he shouldn't. He didn't know. He wished she hadn't gone to her mom's.

She was back again. "Petunias," she said.

"What?"

"The nursery lady, Paula. You know Paula. She ordered some...she has some pots for me. I meant to pick them up. It's no big deal, but she's got that temper thing. We don't get those flowers, they're done for. She'll burn them."

"Petunias."

"Yeah, little—can you picture them? Little flowers. It doesn't matter, Paula's got them. Ask for Becky's flowers."

"Pick up petunias."

"You got it, thank you. And it has to be today."

"Hey Beck," he said, but she was addressing her mom again. He watched the rain.

"Sorry, what?" she said.

"Nothing."

"No, tell me."

"You're just...you're great. I miss you."

"Okay."

For some reason, that'd been what he'd needed to say.

"I miss you, too," she said.

"Petunias."

He felt an odd caution, stepping into the garage and seeing his car there, waiting in the dark like a patient thing in a shrouded cage. Yet also it just was his car. If he sat in it, he could drive through town like an ordinary citizen. He punched the switch. The garage door shuddered and hummed.

If he sensed, driving to the nursery, what terrible things he might do with the vehicle, it was only as he'd sensed, years ago, the terrible depth of a frozen lake where he'd played, the ice creaking underfoot. It was there, okay, but he wasn't in it, he was above. As he'd walked the ice then, his arms sideways, his steps flat and ginger, so he drove now, his palms soft on the wheel, his foot easing the accelerator, lifting, easing the brake. It was how he thought, too. He thought loose thoughts, low-impact. Downtown glided by, and then the buildings past downtown, then trees. He followed the highway, tapping his wheel to a song.

Coastland Tree and Garden was a series of greenhouses behind which lay long rows of orderly plant life. The few times he'd been there he'd liked it. Becky had hunted for stuff, and he'd wandered the tables, breathing the wet air and splashing his fingers through leaves. It had a nice feeling, a good greenhouse, the whirring fans like something Buddhist, like a hum.

He walked inside. There were people there, but no Paula, so he stopped at a table and browsed. The plants he touched were low, flowerless things with broad leaves the color of watermelon skin. They gripped his fingers. Farther down he found tall, spiny blooms that were like formations he'd seen in tide pools.

At the end of the row, he turned and came down another. There he found smaller pots whose flowers were just stabs of color, hundreds of them, above which drooped ropy blooms, resembling braids of garlic. At a certain point, a thin pipe hissed water on things. Everything was so even and regimented, and fresh, that he forgot his terrible morning. He came to the front and saw Paula, but wasn't ready to bother her. He turned down another row. What a nice ten minutes it was.

When it came back, it was the plants that did it, or was their ordering and arrangement. Or it was the secure feeling that order and arrangement inspired. In any case, strolling down a row, it occurred to John he could mess everything up. There was no reason to. In fact he actively wished not to—the place was soothing and peaceful. All the same he could do it, it was within his power. He was thirty-two years old. Nothing in those years indicated he was capable of mindless criminality, but if he desired he could swipe pots from a table, could send them crashing. What'd stop him? It was that capacity that made destroying the nursery so awful to consider, and so alluring.

What he saw first, and vividly, was his arm encircling some pots and raking them down. He heard the crash, and saw clay shards skate the floor. Next, he stomped the shards, and shouted at them. He kicked the table and over it went. From the rubble, he fished a jagged shard and drew it down his palm, the flesh opening like a zippered jacket, so that what'd been the murmured confusion of bystanders became hysterical screams, a stampede for the doors.

The pipe stopped hissing. He stood among the plants, trying to feel his hands as his own, as instruments guided by sane calculation. It was time to go. He walked up front and stood in line at the register. Why was he there again? Pontoons or something. Platoons. Paula had a pot on the desk and was explaining things to a man in white jeans. The man turned a leaf and indicated the underside, and Paula nodded and turned another leaf. They nodded together, their fists in the leaves. That he, John, was a customer like any customer, proceeding through the errands of a day—that wasn't lost on him. He was absorbed in the membrane of things. But rather than support him, that membrane invited savagery. He watched the man in white jeans.

Picture it, he thought. At the nursery inquiring as to some point of horticulture, the nursery and people in it as plain as sky, when from the midst of that plainness reaches a hand. The man's windpipe, John understood, would be rent from his neck before he realized the day no longer was normal, that something had ruptured, there'd been a breach. God, but the man would be confused. Everyone would be confused, and into that confusion, deeper and deeper, he, John, would grind them. Paula'd move for the door, for a safety which by then had lifted away like the tethers of a balloon, and he with his own hands would drag her back, would emphasize the reality of this unreal event. Behind the desk were trowels, pruners, wire…

He made it out and into the car and hauled down the highway, but it stayed with him, the fever of it. He gripped the wheel hard, gripped his jaws, tooth on tooth. Jesus, he thought, Jesus, and fought the knowledge that a man's eyes needn't stay open while he drove a motor vehicle. No physical law enforced that. He shut them quickly, mostly a blink, but then shut them longer, and longer, and jammed the gas. Jesus, he thought, flying at the dark.

Sunday, he left bed only to urinate and drink water before returning again, the shades drawn. Monday was better. He woke with the conviction he was an uncomplicated man capable only of his life's tasks. Still, he called in sick to work. Then he called Steve.

John and Steve had grown up together, and been friends despite sharing nothing in common and being nothing alike, or else had been friends on account of that. Each was so fully not the other that they'd developed a kind of removed appreciation, like how a person stands back to admire artwork. Starting in junior high, when John was learning piano, Steve had begun and never ceased accumulating psychological ailments, until he'd acquired every disorder known to John, and a great many not known. Steve was a troubled guy, was the short of it. But he'd held on. He had some job or other. He was sitting with his hands in his lap when John arrived at the restaurant and dropped his keys on the table.

Steve watched him get comfortable in the chair and roll back his sleeves. "Captain John," he said.

"Steve."

"Cruising the galaxy. Assisting indigenous populations."

Steve had a way of speaking where what he said had no literal meaning, which John assumed was a symptom of his other problems. When Steve spoke, John didn't always have something to add.

They sat a moment, Steve watching him.

"Work okay?" John said finally, but it was too late. Steve had detected something. "What's going on here?" his friend said.

"What?" John said.

"What?"

"I don't know what you…"

"He doesn't know what I mean." Steve looked off and drew a breath. "John, don't make a career of lying. It doesn't suit you."

He didn't know what to say.

"Out with it," Steve said.

He tried to think how he could explain it, and still was thinking when the waitress arrived and asked for their order. They weren't ready, Steve said, and the waitress withdrew.

John still was thinking. Steve lowered his face to catch John's gaze.

"I don't know how to put this," John said.

"Are you coming out? Is that what this is?"

"Steve…"

"I don't care how you swing, John."

"Okay."

"Not that I'm a sally. Though I could be a sally. These things are never clear."

They sat awhile.

Steve said, "John, if you're…"

"Do you ever think about things?" he said.

"Do I…what do you mean?"

"Things." John looked around. "Like you're sitting here. Do you ever…?"

"This isn't enough information to understand what you're saying," Steve said.

When he couldn't think how to put it, he drew breath and simply told the thing outright, beginning to end. He described the cliff and the drive home, and then the nursery and the drive home from that. He said he hadn't left the house. He was worried for when Becky got back. "I'll do something, I know it. I mean not really, but I could. That's the thing. I mean I could just…" His hand was over the table, gesturing. He thought why not, and slammed it down. He slammed it again, harder, so that their glasses leapt. Steve, his expression unchanged, lifted the glasses until the table settled, then set them down again.

People nearby had glanced over, then glanced elsewhere as if the commotion at John and Steve's table were simply on the natural circuit of glancing. John continued in a lower voice, "And it could keep going. I don't know what'd stop it, Steve. And then what? It'd be done, you know? I'd have done it. Then what?"

Steve sipped his water. "Okay."

"What would I do, Steve? I'd have done it. It'd be real."

"That's right," Steve said.

John had suspected his friend was crazy, but now knew it. The man was smiling for Christ's sake. *Smiling*. His hand lingered at his mouth, as if to conceal it, but it was in his eyes. Then he broke out in laughter.

"Are you crazy?" John said.

Steve shook his head, but then nodded, but then shook his head. "Christ."

At last, Steve managed a breath. "John."

"This isn't funny."

"No. Nothing is funny. I agree."

The hell was he talking about? John wondered.

"Look," Steve said, "you're fine."

"I know that. What I'm saying is…"

"No, I know what you're saying. You're fine. It goes away."

"Goes away."

"It will. I promise."

But then Steve laughed again, apologizing with his hands.

"You're crazy," John said.

"Me?" Steve croaked. He clapped a hand on his chest. "*Me?*"

"You're laughing!"

"John, I'm just...hey, I'm proud of you!"

"*Proud?*"

"I mean isn't it great? Captain John, happier than a speeding bullet, leaping uncertainty in a single bound. Except they shouldn't have given you x-ray vision."

"Can you say what you mean? You talk like shit."

"You've got bigger problems than how I talk, boy, trust me. But it fades, John. You're fine."

The waitress came and laid silverware before them. Steve eyed John and slid the knives out of reach. Then he laughed and laughed.

Wrecking his car or smashing clay pots, even cutting his hand with those pots or cutting people, or ending people or ending himself—awful as that all was, those thoughts didn't bother him so much as the thought of Becky's return, and what might happen. He would devote his full self to the prevention of it, but it might happen anyway. Then it'd be done. It was Tuesday afternoon. He bustled through the house, wondering how to protect her. Only what could he do? She was his wife. At night, they undressed and lay skin on skin. Always, there would be only him and her, and anything flowing him-to-her would have only him to staunch it.

Again he passed through the house, from the upstairs bedrooms to the basement, and then through the kitchen and living room. The movement itself acquired a tone of preparation, and so he kept it up, though finally it was useless. He stood at the window. The garage door lurched and Becky pulled into the drive.

When she came in the kitchen he was sitting in the living room. It'd seemed like the thing to do, as if by withdrawing from his feet he might also withdraw a little into his skin, might retreat from his hands. There his hands lay in his lap, a pulse throbbing his knuckles. It was a life, that pulse, was a force trying to lift his hands into use, but against that force he applied his hands' weight and pinned everything down. He was still.

"Babe?" She leaned her head in the room.

"Hey."

"What're you doing?"

"I'm fine," he said.

"All right…"

Exhaling, he imagined his lungs as a kind of repository for his mind, a pit where he might be quarantined. He stayed there.

"So I'm back from my mom's," Becky said.

He was breathing, was fine. But what he'd do to her grew then from whatever recess of himself it'd retreated to and lifted flush with his skin, so that he felt it there, humming his nerves. He fought it back, but then it rose again until, just a little, it exceeded his skin. The shape of his act opened before him, as a kind of vacuum into which he leaned, just perceptibly. There was something he'd do. He'd fill the act, with his hands, like gloves of air.

"John?"

Jesus, he thought, Jesus this was it. The sounds at that moment, the trickle of water in pipes, the tick and hush of the furnace, were the actual, true sounds of an actual instant in time when this terrible thing would transpire. His pulse spread from his hands, was in his throat, his ears.

"John, are you okay?"

He pushed to his feet and crossed the room. He should say hello, should kiss and move his arms around her, but something somewhere had detached, and John now was less acting than watching unfold an act he already, sadly, had initiated.

"Hey," she breathed, and kissed him. She wrapped his neck in her arms. And this was it now. This was the moment. As it stood, things were ordinary and intimate. But she was too close, too exposed, the moment too thin. In an instant he'd perforate it, and their past together, their life and feeling…

She kissed him again, and patted his chest. She moved off through the kitchen.

It was as if he'd fallen, as if he'd toed the ledge and inclined his weight past all hope of retrieval, only to have the chasm vanish and leave him stumbling on flat earth. Becky went to the car and returned with sacks of groceries. She heaved them onto the table and unloaded cans and jars.

At this new remove, she was a whole, complete thing, a woman at work. What'd been a vulnerable closeness, a warmth he might at any moment destroy, now was a scene he might consider calmly, and enter. Deliberately, like a man operating dangerous machinery, he crossed to the grocery sacks and withdrew a canned soup. There it lay in his hand. He was holding soup was all. He crossed and placed it on a shelf. Passing Becky, he patted her hip. Just that. He opened his palm, and let it rest a moment on her jeans. For all the smallness of the gesture, he was buried in it, and safe.

By the time the sacks were empty and folded under the sink, he was safer still. Anyways, he was calm. What remained of his earlier state was only a blank exhaustion, like how you felt, they said, after a seizure.

Becky glanced around the kitchen, smacking her palms.

"All set?" he said.

"You make it over there?"

"Over...?" He had no idea what she meant.

"The flowers?"

"I don't know what you're talking about," he said.

"The flowers?"

Then he remembered. "Petunias."

She melted in a slump, and dropped her chin on her chest.

"Jesus, I'm sorry," he said.

"She'll feed those flowers to the wolves, John. Wolves." But as if sensing that this, the two of them, was at that moment all he could give her, she let it go. "Hey, okay. It's flowers, big deal." She said, "We'll be good, I think, babe. We'll survive."

Steve was right, it turned out. A day came he didn't think about it, then two days and three. A week passed. When he thought about it next he was in the kitchen chopping carrots. The knife was in hand. Becky appeared and kissed his cheek, and like a flood the scene rose in him, the pivot and thrust, the rip and instant of recognition, everything irreparable…but like a flood it receded and there he remained at the counter, lifting and pushing the blade.

He thought about it a few days later, and again the following week, then not for a while.

They were safe. He wouldn't do anything. But even when weeks passed and nothing weighed any heavier on his mind than petunias or carrots, there persisted in him some gravity that was less knowledge than what lay under knowledge, the way living is less blood than what runs in the blood, a pulse. After a seizure, they said you felt a certain way, felt empty and dead, and this was like that, except there never had been a seizure and so the feeling never quite had started. And yet it never quite stopped.

He was fragile these days. One afternoon, he stood at the window watching Becky pull weeds, and when she came inside and peeled off her handkerchief, he apologized. "Beck, I'm sorry," he said.

"Well, I accept. Good." She tossed the handkerchief on the table and wiped her palms on her jeans. She watched him awhile. "That all?" she said.

"I'm sorry," he said again.

"John, when people apologize there's usually a reason…"

Though maybe what he'd lost was just that, that assumption things stayed how they were until some reason made them otherwise. That'd been a good assumption, he realized now. It'd made for nice hikes. Whereas today, he couldn't imagine cliffs. Gusty winds, slick rock. Think what swirled in that gray air, gray matter, while reason like the rest of us waited with nervous hands, hoping to catch whatever grew heavy suddenly, like a stone, and fell.

ABOVE IT ALL

FOR ALL OUR FIGHTING ABOUT WHERE TO LIVE (I wanted Tokyo, Lena wanted Boston), we actually both wound up in Seattle. Or I'd heard she was in Seattle. After our split, I didn't keep up with her. It was funny. Our fights about where to live had been vicious. Boston, she'd said, was the intellectual capital of the world. She couldn't understand why I didn't want to live in the world's intellectual capital. For me, Tokyo was about liberation. A person didn't need to live where he came from, not in the city he came from, nor in the country or hemisphere. You could be what you wanted. Tokyo was as much about declaring that as it was about the bright lights and pagodas. So we went our separate ways, or believed we had, until we ended up in Seattle.

I'm married now, and have a son, so when I heard Lena was in town I wasn't going to do anything about it. I'm not a sleaze. But Seattle isn't big (no Tokyo, certainly), and I knew eventually we'd run into each other. It got to where I saw her at the store and post office, and on sidewalks downtown, any blonde in a crowd. I imagined when we did meet there'd be mutual embarrassment. We'd both capitulated. As I envisioned it, we'd cross paths by the Space Needle, that most intransigent Seattle image, and hang our heads, having been caught in the same lie.

Instead, we ran into each other at the gym on SPU's campus. I was with my wife, Freddie, and our son, Braden, who was attending SPU's basketball camp. It was the end of the week, when they hold the tournament. I saw a woman who looked like Lena, but was so used to seeing such women I didn't react. She looked down the bleachers at us and still I didn't do anything (I can disappear in my head sometimes). She lifted her hands, like *Hey? Hello?*

"Oh shit," I said.

"What?" Freddie said.

Lena came down the bleachers. "Um, Mark Hagen."

I hugged her. "Lena."

"Someone said you lived here."

"This is Freddie," I said.

They shook hands.

"What're you doing here?" Lena said.

"I'm an attorney."

"I mean at camp."

Lena and Freddie swapped glances, like *Is he spacey or what?* A lot of people have swapped that glance about me. "Our son's playing," I said. I pointed him out, a big kid with big knees and feet. He set a pick that knocked another kid over, but by the time he rolled to the bucket someone had already scored.

"I see the resemblance," Lena said.

"Why're you here?"

"Mine…" She pointed at some kids on the sideline, waiting for the next game, "…is dark hair there on the left."

It didn't surprise me she had kids, weird as that was to think about. Kids had been something we'd agreed on, even if we'd used them as instruments in other arguments. Her kids needed exposure to the best and brightest (Boston), while mine needed broader perspectives (Tokyo).

"God, this is nuts," Lena said.

"Yeah."

"Are you guys free later? We could grab lunch?"

"Oh…" Freddie looked at me. "Braden has his thing."

"What thing?"

"The lunch? The team thing?" She glanced helplessly at Lena.

"I guess we'll raincheck," I said.

"No," Freddie said, "you go."

"We have that thing."

"I'll handle it. You go."

"You sure?"

She touched Lena's arm. "Just be sure he looks both ways before crossing the street."

It wasn't just the two of us. I came in the restaurant and saw Lena with her kid, another kid, and a man I guessed was her husband. He was handsome, but not as handsome as he could've been, which helped.

"Well hey," she said. "Guys, this is Mark."

I waved at the kids, and shook the husband's hand.

"We knew each other in Chicago. And Mark, this is Todd. This is Luke and Lindsey."

"Nice to meet you."

"We were just talking about Chicago, actually."

"Yeah?"

"We took Luke and Lindsey in May. They're little travel hounds. We saw the aquarium. What else did we see?"

"The fishes," Lindsey said. She was five or so, and playing with her napkin.

"That was the aquarium," her brother said.

"Nah-uh, it was the shed. They keep the fish in the shed."

The family laughed, which the girl enjoyed.

"What else?" Lena said. "There were museums. We went to baseball games. There was Mommy's school."

"Vampires!" Lindsey cried.

Lena said, "She thought Harper Library was Dracula's castle. But no, it was fun. We liked Chicago. It was our warm-up for New York."

A waitress arrived and unloaded a tray of waters, and I thought about the previous summer when Freddie and Braden had gone to Spain. Lena was so proud of her globetrotting family. She should know when my family traveled they went to Europe, but there was no way to weave that into the conversation. I sipped my water. "Harper Library," I said.

"Old Harper. They've got Suzzallo here, but it's no Harper."

When I'd known her, Lena was in her second year of a combined MD/PhD in social psychology, a ludicrously pretentious degree path. She'd planned to be a research psychiatrist, and apparently had become one, though for all her expertise in behavior and cognition she wasn't very subtle about baiting me into asking about her job. "Suzzallo?" I said. "Is that UW?"

"Yeah."

"So you're teaching?"

The waitress returned and stood between Lena and me, but Lena couldn't wait. She leaned around the waitress. "Well, it's not teaching. You give lectures, but it's a research appointment. That's the side I'm on."

I could've responded, but instead smiled at the waitress and ordered a sandwich. When she was gone, I said, "You were saying?"

"Oh, nothing. It's just not really teaching. Todd's on the teaching side of things. He's in engineering."

"Is that right?"

Todd sipped his water. "I engineer sabbaticals."

"Oh, stop it," Lena said. "That's his favorite joke."

"It's a subspecialty," Todd said.

We laughed and Lindsey said, "Sub sandwich specialty," and we laughed harder, the light pouring through the windows and the restaurant alive with chatter and the tinkling of silverware, and I thought: I hope these assholes know how much I make, and how people in the real world look down on academics. I hope they know I'm above them.

Todd said, "And you're an attorney?"

"I am."

"What area?"

"Litigation. And we do international and admiralty stuff."

"Admiralty? Like maritime law?"

"Yeah."

"Mark wanted to live abroad," Lena said. "Was it Japan? He has an international interest."

You cunt, I thought, sipping my water.

By the time the food came, we were back on them. "So our summers are pretty light. At least for Todd," Lena said. "He's got three months."

I drew the toothpick from my sandwich. "That's nice."

"It is for a while," Todd said.

"How do you pass the time?"

"I play solitaire."

"Stop it," Lena said.

"I shoot spitwads."

"He does tons of stuff. He's a reader. And he's into triathlons now."

"Yeah?"

Todd shrugged. "It's something to do."

Lena poked at her salad. My guess, she'd eat two bites and waste the rest. She said, "Todd's modest, he's an athlete. He ran at Wisconsin."

"No kidding?"

"Well, but I wasn't an athlete. I was fast, but I wasn't athletic." He nodded at Luke. "Luke's the athlete."

I looked at their son. He was Braden's age or so, a frail kid with soft skin. I decided he was no athlete. He was from defective stock. "How's camp?" I asked him.

He shrugged, working a fry in some ketchup.

"They're in the championship," Lena said.

"Yeah? Wait, how old are you? Braden's in the championship."

"He's eleven," Lena said.

I wondered how good of an athlete he could be if his mom fielded all his questions. Lena rooted in her purse and took out a bracket. "What's your son's team?" she said.

I didn't know. "Who're they playing?"

"The Sounders?"

That was it. It was the Sounders or Hawks or something. "That's Braden," I said. "Seven-thirty?"

Lena consulted the schedule. "Seven."

"That's Braden."

"Well," she poked her salad, "that's awkward. Maybe we shouldn't eat together."

"Maybe not," I said. I pretended to go to the bathroom, and paid the bill.

They had the afternoon off, but Braden's coach wanted them at the gym, watching other games. They sat in the bleachers with the blank expressions they showed the world, Braden with the expression he'd shown me for years, the slack mouth and eyes. Now and again a secret passed among them, spreading grins like wind combing a field, before whistling off and leaving them dead-faced. I watched from the opposite bleachers. Freddie was somewhere running errands. Between games, I walked over and waved Braden out of the stands. His dead expression became dead and confused, his eyes suspicious, but he came down.

"What're you doing?" I said.

"Watching games."

"Let's shoot around."

"What?"

"Come on, let's go."

"No."

"Let's go," I said.

"Is this father-son bonding?"

"Ha-ha. Come on."

I led him out of the gym and through the halls until we found an empty gym, where there were balls and a water cooler. "Get warmed up," I said.

"What're you talking about?"

"Warm up, let's go." I'd been at work that morning, and was in my loafers and slacks, but trotted the length of the floor. At the other end, I planted and trotted back. I didn't play anymore, but had played at Virginia, which is a better school than Wisconsin, on top of basketball being more serious than track. Track athletes, in my experience, are like paralegals who say paralegal work interests them more than practicing law. Sure it does, pal. Braden watched me, slouched in the baby fat he hadn't grown out of. I tossed him a ball. "Get some shots."

"Dad," he said.

"Let's see it."

My son's big, but hasn't discovered nuance. He dribbled awkwardly and flung the ball both-handed at the backboard. It didn't go in. "Let's see another," I said, and tossed it back to him. His shot was awful, his hands flopping like fish.

"Have they talked about guide hands?" I said.

"Dad, I'm tired."

"The shot actually is one-handed. Give me that." He threw me the ball. He even tried to zip it, throwing it hard from his hip, but he's not strong enough to zip a pass. I made a cradle of my fingers and set the ball on them, like you're supposed to. "See? One-handed. And not on your palm. The other hand," I brought up my left, "just guides it. It doesn't change anything." I shot the ball and bricked it. Braden laughed, but I got the ball back and splashed it through the net. "Your turn."

He dribbled and shot like he always had, his hands crazy.

"One-handed," I said.

"I am."

"No, you're not."

He shot again, the same shit.

"Here." I lifted his hand for him and made the cradle. I set the ball on his fingers. "Like that." When I took my hands away, the ball tumbled off. Braden left his hand up, to show it was my fault.

"Can you not do this?"

"It falls off."

"Try again."

He collected the ball and tried to get it on his fingers. It tumbled off. His next attempt he shot quickly, before the ball could escape, but it'd escaped already and his hand slipped from under it. The ball struck his forehead. I never know with Braden. He fails on purpose sometimes, to make a point, then other times is actually trying and sucks.

"Okay," I said.

"It's not working."

"Your hands are too small. It's fine."

He tried again, and again the ball hit his face. That one was on purpose, but I ignored it.

"We'll find another way."

"Let's go back," he said.

"You don't want to win?"

"The game?"

"It's a championship. Braden, that's an opportunity."

"Dad, it's camp."

"You wouldn't be here if it didn't matter."

He laughed. "You signed me up!"

"Look. Does this feel good?" I poked his stomach.

"Stop it."

"Does it?" I poked him again.

"Dad."

"You can bully or be bullied. Those're the choices."

His face was dead again.

"This is how you do it." I carried the ball to the top of the key. "What are you that no one else is?"

"What?"

"Think about yourself. You're something no one else is. What is it?"

"I don't know."

"You're big, Braden. So make it about bigness. Here." I threw him the ball and walked around so I stood between him and the basket. "I'm bigger than you. Can you score on me?"

"I'll score on you."

"Do it," I said.

He started dribbling, the way kids do while they figure out their move. I stood there. I didn't get in defensive stance, didn't do anything with my hands. I might've been standing in an elevator. Finally Braden drove. He jerked around like he was fast, but he wasn't. I took one step, and when he shot I swatted the ball into some folding chairs. "Go get it," I said.

Braden glared at me. It was good to see some anger in him. He got the ball and brought it back. This time when he drove I stepped in front of him. He tried the other direction but I was there, too. After some dribbling he shot a jumper, but with Braden you saw the shot coming five seconds in advance. I tipped the ball and controlled it. I dribbled to the top of the key, or rather walked alongside the bouncing ball, unbuttoning my cuffs. "Now I'm going to score on you," I said.

He was mad. He bent at the waist with his arms outstretched, a pathetic defensive stance.

"Not because I'm better," I said. "Because I'm bigger."

"Fuck you," he said.

"Whoa!" I laughed. "Okay!"

"I'm going to beat you."

"No, you won't. I'm bigger, Braden."

Unbuttoning the cuffs hadn't been necessary. I turned my back and just walked Braden down, dribbling where he couldn't reach it. He leaned against me, first with an arm bar and then just pounding his shoulder in my ribs, but nothing helped. I backed him down, step by step. As he heaved against me, I spoke softly over my shoulder, "It's size, son. I'm not doing anything you can't do. I'm dribbling. Can you dribble?" We were almost to the basket. "I'm even going to shoot like you," I said. "Two-handed. I'll miss one like you, too. It won't matter. I'm bigger. This is about size."

When we reached the bucket, I turned and flung up some bullshit. It hit off the backboard, but I was bigger and got the rebound. "I'll miss another. Watch." I did, and got the rebound. "One of these'll go in. I just have to be bigger." On the fourth or fifth shot, Braden threw himself into me as I heaved forward. It knocked him down. "Bigger," I said, and tossed the ball through the net.

When he got to his feet he was sniffling, trying not to cry. "Personally?" I said. "I'd rather be the bully."

Lena and Todd are so clever. Luke's team was the Bulls, so after lunch they'd gone to the mall and bought us all (the two of them and Lindsey, and me and Freddie) matching Chicago Bulls shirts. We had a good laugh. "You don't have to wear them," Lena said. "But you should."

We sat together in the third row. I dropped the shirt at my feet.

After our shootaround, Braden had been hurt like I'd not seen him hurt in years, cracked open and whimpering, but that was gone now and he was trotting through lay-ins. "Is he okay?" Freddie said.

"Bray?" I said. "Why?"

"He looks different."

"He's focused," I said.

They blew the horn, and the teams collected at their benches. As they took the floor, the crowd applauded and whistled. It was a good turnout for a camp championship. Lena, who sat next to me, said in my ear, "Should we make a bet?"

"I wouldn't do that to you," I said.

She leaned back, still clapping, and regarded me. "Mister Cocky," she said.

It was out of character, or at least wasn't the kind of thing I'd done before, but I said in Lena's ear, "I'm just better than you, Leens. Sorry."

It was nice, because there was no varnish then. All the friendly bullshit vanished, and she looked coldly at the court. "Fuck you," she muttered.

"You certainly have. You loved it."

Todd's face leaned into view. "What's going on down there?"

"Nothing, Todd," I said.

The game started, Luke's team controlling the tip and Lena pig-whistling and clapping, never mind that Luke was on the bench. They scored the first bucket and she leapt to her feet. Half her applause was for the court, and then she leaned and applauded in my face. You poor cunt, I thought. She'd won the moment, but strength is strength and wins out.

It was late in the half before Braden got the ball. He didn't do anything, but then got the ball again and remembered my instruction. He lowered a shoulder and bulldozed the kid in front of him. It wasn't Luke, but it was good enough. He slopped one off the backboard, two points. The next time he missed the shot, but so many defenders were required to box him out that his teammate got the rebound and scored.

He committed turnovers and charges, but by the second half Braden had acquired inevitability, like the heavy thing he was tumbling downhill, accelerating. Lena'd shut up, of course, though Todd still had his manners. His face leaned into view. "You've got a rhinoceros there, Mark."

"What can I say?" I said. "We're athletes."

"I guess so." He was a friendly enough guy, but Lena hissed something sharp in his ear and that was the last we heard from Todd. I hope he does all right, that engineering professor, but also I hope Lena's ashamed of him the rest of her life. She should be. She had a chance at something better.

The moment I'd hoped for came with two minutes left. I was worried it wouldn't happen, but then Braden set a screen, there was a switch, and the kid guarding him was Luke. "Hey Leens?" I said.

She ignored me.

"Sorry for this," I said.

The ball reversed to Bray. Poor Luke had a sound defensive stance, and seemed an earnest enough kid, but his parents had disadvantaged him by being his parents. Braden plowed him over. He just burst through the kid like a door he knocked down. They called a charge, but so what? "Whoops," I said. The ref lifted a hand while Luke rocked on the floor and finally struggled to his feet. There were two minutes left, but that did it. Lena stepped over Todd and picked up Lindsey. She walked off. Todd looked around, then shrugged at me and followed her.

"Where're they going?" Freddie said.

"We weren't wearing their shirts," I said.

The Sounders won easily, by ten or so, and were SPU camp champions. It was a light, wonderful feeling, a good feeling for all. Freddie was happy. When we got to him, Braden was smiling. I took his team out for pizza.

It was driving home, crossing the Aurora Bridge, that I realized I'd never see Lena again. Or I'd see her at the airport or post office, and it'd be like not seeing her. She'd refuse to know me. Whatever. I was better than she was. It was farther on, passing through downtown, that I realized Braden was saying something, or Freddie. Or they were talking to each other. They had their thing going, the two of them. And my thing, whatever it was, had always been something else.

A PLACE TO CROSS

IN THE BOOKS HE READ, tortured characters always went fishing. The nature-immersion restored their gritty serenity, which catharted all pain. When Bethany left him, he didn't fish immediately. He took an apartment downtown, and for a month lingered in bars, hoping some kind of woman would approach him, or that he'd discover a woman alone, and utter words to charm her. Instead, he drank to infirmity. No one went to bars alone, except him, and the people in groups were too busy with their own conversations to engage a stranger. The nights devolved into nightmarish teacup rides, hysterical faces lurching past. Until he realized his was the hysterical face, the lurching one; the other faces were calm in their booths. Mornings, he couldn't believe himself. I'm a vampire, he told his pillow, a vampire. He was glad his evening had failed, glad he was alone, unfettered by the stench and habits of some sad barfly. He vowed to stay sober awhile, and healthy, but the sun rose and fell and by evening he levitated from his coffin, the bar lights agleam in his eyes.

A morning came he thought he'd hang himself. He even toyed the belt in his fingers, like a buyer of exotic silks. That's when he decided he'd go fishing.

He piled everything in his car, and on his way out of town bought extras of everything, even an extra rod. He couldn't afford an extra rod, but Bethany's departure had revised his budgeting. Formerly, he'd had a checking account for daily expenses, a savings account for medium-range expenses, such as vacations and car repairs, a 401k for retirement, and a credit card for emergencies. Now, every penny he laid hands to was for buying his way out of heartache. The apartment downtown, for instance, was double the mortgage of his old place, the place he and Bethany had shared. Twice already he'd settled a bar tab by emptying his wallet onto the counter, like a piggy bank.

Spokane disappeared in his rearview, like a shabby Atlantis going under, and then he passed Coeur d'Alene, with its majestic lake. Coeur d'Alene always had captivated him, though recently he'd distrusted beauty. Not because it evaporated (Bethany), but because he was barely hanging on, and if he opened himself to beauty's power it might sever the last threads. He drove on, ignoring vistas. At a gas station up the river he bought hot dogs and chips, lots of each. The cooler next to the hot dogs offered beer, and every time he glanced at it he swept more franks into his basket, as if to anchor his thirst.

The campsite he chose was farther on, way farther, where you could lob a stone from one riverbank to the other. His tent was simple, but he couldn't master it. No matter his adjustments, one side drooped like the flag of a defeated nation. Fuck it. The weather was immaculate, clear and breezy. He had the campground to himself. At his feet lay hours of good fishing, but he crawled in the tent and lay face down on his sleeping bag.

His name was Mitchell O'Connor. Each night of his thirty-six years had delivered him to the shore of breaking day, but like his life's other patterns, that was nearing its end.

He woke at dusk with long shadows on the tent walls, like arms seeking one another. That the light had changed was sad and frightening. He crawled out and stretched. Through the trees, by the river, he saw an aspen aflame with dying sunlight, just the one tree, as if its roots far underground had tapped the light of another age, some fossilized radiance.

His car was a tangle of shit, of leader and spilled tins of flies, of hot dogs. He ate a few, like wet breadsticks, and a handful of chips, then hauled everything out in the dirt. He pulled on his waders and assembled tackle. When he'd extracted the necessities, he left the rest where it lay and hacked a path through the brush.

The river where he reached it tumbled off a shoal and swirled through glassy depths, leaving the opposite bank hospitable—it was a gravel bar—and the near bank, at his feet, a treacherous cut dropping vertically to the pool's depths. He gazed up- and downstream, filling his lungs with the rugged tranquility that'd saved Hemingway and Jim Harrison heroes, but also noticing he couldn't cast from this side, with the brush, and on account of the brush couldn't move downstream to an easier place to cross.

He lowered a foot down the bank, but found nowhere to place his toe and withdrew it. He tried the other foot, as if that would improve the terrain. The awkwardness of the moment was painful, and wasn't very Hemingway. As a brash gesture, which seemed required, he stepped back and simply launched from the bank. He landed not far across, the frigidness seizing his lungs and muscles. Putting his feet down, he found a riverbed racing by like a treadmill. He tripped, and lost his rod. Finally he scrambled ashore, his waders sloshing. He worked them off and poured the legs out like gourds. The rod had caught on something and was jutting from the water, opening a seam in the current. He recovered it and found a place to dry off.

With the sun singeing the ridges, the day ending, he got back in his waders and fished. Mitchell never had been a fisherman, not really, despite reading books and mastering the terminology. All the tackle he owned (except for the new rod) had been gifted over the years, from his mother and then from Bethany, and he was too sentimental to use in practical life an object a loved one had given him. This maybe was his fourth time on a river. He waded upstream, working the rod overhead, but his timing was wretched. There was slack in the line, which his casts merely noodled before the whole rigging—fly line, leader, and tippet—collapsed at his knees and carried downstream. Finally he shortened his cast and found power, but he never landed the fly where he wished, or landed it there and found no trout. He kicked upstream. The sun had fallen, though the west-facing mountains still burned with it, like children keeping their chins above water.

He caught a fish, a little one, and decided that was enough. It was dusk now, and smoky in the canyon. He was chilly. But he had only to glance downstream—it did not even require a step that direction—and imagine his limp tent in its empty campground, his slimy franks. He couldn't go back there. Upstream was a narrow chute with dense brush overhanging one bank and the other bank sheer rock. It was impassable, but he waded towards it, keeping to the bank with softer eddies. He was to the chute before he realized he was on the cliff side, with the current too strong to cross. He could wade back and cross downstream, but didn't believe his dubious personal worth warranted such caution.

Up close, the cliff offered fissures and holds, and where the cliff met the water it flattened into tiers of shelving. He made his way along the first shelf, his rod outstretched for balance. The river churned at his feet, lifting and twisting and yet stationary, the same whirls endlessly repeated, the same leaping sprays, its icy draft chilling him. He slipped a little. For all the thundering current, the rock in places was slick with algae, the lapping water hiding and revealing it like a magician's hands. He continued unsteadily. Ahead, the river widened into placid shallows, where if he wished he could spend the whole night, clear to dawn, failing to catch trout.

Instead, he slipped badly and struck his forehead. He didn't lose consciousness, not all the way, but the white shock of impact passed through him and out the other side, carrying with it all the properties of Mitchell O'Connor, and leaving behind just some limp thing, mute and rubbery. The current encircled his calf, and drew him into the river like a duchess selecting a scarf.

When his head cleared he was stumbling up the road, he

didn't know which direction. He was sopping, and had lost his hat and net. Somehow he'd retained his rod. Ahead, in a dark meadow, was a campfire. As he approached, a man stood like a bear and watched him. There were two others at the fire. "Hello!" the man called. "Are you lost?"

It was Peter, his wife Dawn, and their daughter Callie. They were camping this week before Callie started AAU softball. When Mitchell stumbled out of the dark they'd just finished dinner, but Peter went in the cooler and found more brats, which he laid on the fire. They gave him dry clothes, a chair, and tea. Dawn inspected the gash on his forehead. It'd clotted, but when she cleaned it the blood ran. She went in the motor home and returned with bandages. They were a kind family, healthy and whole, and in a better world Mitchell would've drowned before finding them.

Dawn knelt beside him, opening a bandage. Peter, tending the brats, glanced over. "That little thing going to do?"

"It's what we have."

"We have that adhesive. Use that."

Dawn went in the motor home and returned with a small rubber tube. After staunching the blood she ran a line of glue down his gash and pressed it closed. She held it there, gripping his features into a perplexed expression.

Peter gazed at the fire. "I'd say you're one lucky hombre," he said.

"I guess so."

"Things like this, always remember your luck. You might've stayed in that river indefinitely, if you catch my drift."

When Dawn removed her hand, the pinching sensation remained. She peeled open the bandage and pressed it on. Mitchell probed it with his fingers. After a time, Peter lifted a brat from the grill and Callie rose to fetch a bun. She made a plate for him, dressing the sausage with mustard and onions, and adding potato salad. She was pretty, with wide hips that made her shoulders look narrow. She laid the plate on his knee.

It'd been weeks since he'd been hungry, and he wasn't hungry then, but the brat when he bit it popped like a clasp, jetting grease on his lips, and his appetite returned. The family watched him eat, sitting forward in their chairs as if the motion of his jaws were some engrossing tale. When he was finished, Peter said, "So tell us about yourself. Who's this gentleman at our fire?"

It was inconsequential, the kind of question one airline passenger asks another, but no one in weeks had asked Mitchell any questions, consequential or otherwise, and certainly no questions about himself. Peter's query was like a door opening on a winter evening, spilling light, warmth, and faces onto the frigid porch, where Mitchell waited, shivering.

"I'm a teacher," he said. It was true, though since Bethany left he didn't feel like a teacher, or like anything. All that was a dream he'd awoken from. Rather, he'd descended from that, from his true life, into a dream from which he couldn't awake.

"A *teacher*," Peter said with wonder. It was as if he'd never met one. "And what do you teach?"

"English. I'm a high school teacher."

"No kidding? Now that's Callie's subject."

Mitchell looked at Callie, who hadn't until now seemed shy. "You like English?" he said.

Peter said, "She reads everything."

"Dad…"

"She does. Her books are all over. If the house falls down, Cal's books will hold it up."

Dawn nodded at her daughter. "Tell him what you just read."

"What're you talking about?" the girl said.

"The fishing one. With the brothers."

Callie sighed.

"*A River Runs Through It?*" Mitchell asked.

"That's it!" Dawn said. "I knew it had a river. Have you read it? Of course you've read it, you're a teacher. And a fisherman."

"Did you like it?" he asked Callie.

"It was good," she said.

"She loved it," Peter said. He removed the other brat. "It's all she talks about. She's been casting with broomsticks."

"Dad, oh my God," Callie said.

"Well, you have. Hey," he jabbed the tongs at Mitchell, "you could teach her. She wants to learn."

"I'd do that," he said.

"Plus you're an educator. A fisherman and educator."

"Chapter One," Mitchell said, and it was the first joke he'd made in weeks: "Don't head-butt rocks."

They laughed, Callie laughing especially, and their laughter upheld him.

"Have this brat," Peter said.

"I'm okay."

Peter offered it again, then laid the brat aside. "Then I guess it's that time."

"Uh-oh," Dawn said.

Peter reached behind him and came up with a bottle of whiskey. "We don't drink much, but we like a sip by the fire." He winked at Mitchell. "Just a sip."

"No harm there," Mitchell said.

"We don't think so."

Peter took Mitchell's mug and pitched his tea in the fire. He poured some whiskey, then added more. Mitchell had hoped not to drink on this trip, and maybe not drink after, but these were good people, and he wouldn't turn away. Besides, he'd hoped for lots of things in life. He hadn't learned much these past weeks—it'd been just misery, without glimpses at wisdom—but one thing he had learned was you couldn't cling to hope. If you weren't willing to part with hope, it'd part with you and take everything with it.

Peter poured for himself and Dawn, and even poured some for Callie, which he diluted with water. They raised their mugs and drank.

"What else about yourself? Tell us who you are," Peter said.

"It's all boring."

"Oh, I doubt it. Where're you from? That's not boring."

Mitchell said Ohio, and when pressed said more about Ohio. He described the insects and corn, the heat, and finally the day in Columbus his senior year he'd decided to move West. He'd read a lot by then, and had discovered in himself a Western spirit. He explained what that was, how parts of yourself had to be feral, and how you had to be fine with that, gesturing as he spoke and finishing his whiskey and most of another. Peter poured him more, maybe pouring lighter this time, and asked if he was a family man.

The fire snapped and hissed, embers zagging the night. The three of them, his new friends, waited in their chairs. Not even with Bethany, in those days of his moving out, when they'd drifted through the house dividing possessions like zombies, like monsters of mythology condemned to that task—not even then, with her, had he been able to discuss this. The trauma of her leaving had wrecked him and left no firm surface a word might spring from. But between himself and this family there'd opened a channel. He could flow to them, and by flowing transfer himself, and divide his heart equally among them. He said, "I was a family man until recently. She left."

Dawn clicked her tongue. "Oh, Mitchell."

That was all he'd planned to say. He'd wished only to share that fact. But there was silence, his friends were listening, and it simply was physics: the high density of his grief flowed to the cavity of their attention. "We met in school," he said, "in Ohio. I knew the moment I saw her I'd get her or fall apart. Frankly, I thought I'd fall apart. She was too good for me. But she saw something in me, or I was so...probably she saw what it'd take to fight me off and gave up. Anyways, we got together. We had years, just *years* we were happy."

Peter was listening, they all were listening. Even Mitchell listened. He both delivered the story and opened his hands to receive it.

"Anything that would happen," he said, "would happen to both of us. I just knew that. Something can't happen to part of something, it happens to all of it. Then I looked away, I don't know. By the time I looked back, she wasn't there. I wasn't there, either, if that makes sense. I'd become something with her. With that gone, I was leftovers."

Dawn touched his arm. "Mitchell."

Losing Bethany was the sadness of his life, but he'd spoken it now, or some version of it, and felt better. "Thank you," he said.

"Shoot," Peter said. "Don't thank us. That's why there's more than one of us on this planet. That's the point."

"I came to the right fire."

"Well, we're glad to have you." Peter filled his mug, then filled Dawn's and Callie's, his own. He tapped his mug against Mitchell's. "Better days ahead. You hang in there."

His drink finished, Mitchell stood to leave, but whether from drunkenness or from his injury, he wobbled and sat. "I think," Peter pushed to his feet, "we'll keep you here tonight."

"I'll go," he said, but Peter disappeared in the motor home and returned with a foam pad and sleeping bag, and a pillow. He spread the bedding near the fire. "You cozy up. In the morning, you can teach us to fish."

After some hugs and good wishes, the three of them went inside. Mitchell crawled in the bag.

His dreams since Bethany left had been horrid scenes of ropes and trapdoors, or else normal scenes with normal furniture, until he discovered at the dream's conclusion all the furniture had been imagined, and the room was vacant. In one dream he stacked plates in a box, only they wouldn't lay evenly. The plates stood on end, or at angles, clanking and tumbling out, shattering on the floor. But in this new dream, the dream opening from his center, Bethany lay on a quilt under a pear tree. Rather she sat, her legs beneath her, the blossoms tangling her hair. He was with her, they could see each other, but a distance had opened between them, and was widening. Still, there was no sadness. The light and silence held a peace, a sense not that things were whole, but that the two of them would share forever the ways things weren't whole, and not lose touch.

It was a good dream. It promised, at thirty-six, Mitchell had bright years ahead, years to become something new and strong. All the same it was a dream, and lives aren't measured in years. At thirty-six or twenty, or at fifty-six or eighty: there are things we don't unbecome, no matter the decades allotted for it, and when those things end so do we.

She was at the campfire, though the fire was dead. She sat in the moonlight. It was part of his dream, but then he emerged from the dream and she was there. "What're you doing?" he said.

Callie glanced at him, then at the sky. "I like the moon."

"I can't see it."

"Come here."

He was drunk, but managed to free himself from the bag and wrap it over his shoulders. He sat beside her.

"It isn't full," she whispered. "Full was yesterday. It's waning."

He studied the moon, and the clouds it bleached. "It looks full."

"It's waning," she said.

After a time, Mitchell said, "You know you guys saved me. I mean that."

"We didn't save you."

"Sure you did."

"You just showed up."

He watched her there, watching the moon. "So," he said, "broomsticks."

Her eyes closed. She was embarrassed.

"It's okay," he said. "That's how you become something, you imagine it. I used to practice with those window blind thingies, the laths."

"No you didn't."

It was true, he'd never done that, but he'd moved into a space where what he wished was so. "I did," he said. "In college. I tied shoestrings to the tip and practiced in the halls."

"You must've been popular."

"I became a fisherman. That's what counts."

They sat together, the moon supervising their silence. He said, "Let's try it."

"Try…?"

"Let's go fishing."

"*Now?*"

"Night's the best time. Let's do it."

She eyed him skeptically.

"Did you read *The Brothers K?* The David Duncan book? I bet you did, didn't you?"

She didn't say anything.

"There's that scene he fishes all night. You remember it."

"It's too cold," she said.

"We're already cold. We might as well fish."

He crossed the campsite to his rod and vest. Callie watched from her chair, but then unfolded and stood. "What do I need?" she said.

"Nothing. Just yourself."

He led her through the meadow, the grass gripping his shins. As he walked, he offered over his shoulder bits of advice, most of it lifted from *A River Runs Through It.* "Casting's ten and two, it's about rhythm," he said. "And it's art, it requires respect."

He let her catch up, then added for fun: "And watch out for wolves."

She poked his ribs. "Shush."

They'd reached the cottonwoods along the water, a thick copse with tangled underbrush. They couldn't see, but could hear the river. "Stay close through here," he said.

"Don't get ahead of me."

He touched her back, leading her through the trees while the moon watched through the canopy, like a shifting eye, and when they reached the river she was holding his hand. They stood at the bank, the moon marbling the water. "Well," he said. "Get in."

Her other hand gripped his arm. "Get *in?*"

"You've read the books. You know how it goes."

"I can't get in there."

He laid the rod aside, and with Callie still grasping his arm rolled his sweatpants over his knees. They were Peter's sweatpants, the ones they'd given him. She let go and rolled up her own sweats. "If I fall," she said, "you'd better catch me."

"I will," he said.

They waded into the current, Callie again on his arm, but made it only a few yards before the water reached her sweats. She pulled them higher, and that got them another yard, but she was too short.

"Hold on," she said, and returned to the bank. In the moonlight, she pressed down her sweats and stepped out of them. Another day, another month or year, Mitchell would've averted his gaze, but he was with this girl. He observed her firm legs, her hips, the delta of pink panties. She waded back to him, the black water encircling her thighs. "If you even think about telling Dad…"

"I won't."

"Taking my pants off with you."

They waded into the current, then stopped and he paid out line. "Let's get you in front of me," he said, and moved behind her.

"Where do I hold it?"

He moved his arms over hers, and fitted her hand on the cork. Her other hand he moved to the line. "Remember it's rhythm," he said, and drew their cast. Her arm had its own intentions, wanting a certain angle and tempo, but he overruled her arm and after some false casts she relaxed and allowed his guidance.

They cast, cast after cast, she pressing against him and he against her, until he released the line at nothing at all, at darkness. His hand moved under her sweatshirt and up her stomach. She whimpered as he cupped her. He kissed her shoulder and neck. She offered her mouth.

On the bank then, on flattened grass, he removed everything from their bodies, opening a smoothness between them. He'd lost Bethany. The man he'd been had died. But over that death a new man formed, a new radiance, and to that radiance he now devoted himself, pressing and biting. How couldn't he? He passed into it, spirit and flesh.

What particular act forced her retreat, what transgression, he couldn't have said. It all was one act, one necessary frontier. But she withdrew. She scooted away, whispering something urgently. But his death yawned beneath them. He clutched at her, at her hips and cunt. She fought him off, screaming and slapping his face, but he wouldn't go back where he'd been. Not there. He cuffed her little throat, and fucked her.

When fundamental realities are voided, all others are tenuous. What can be true when greater truths crumble? For a month he'd swum in that vagary, where anything at any moment could become real or not, where nothing was firm. Only Callie's crying and bloodied mouth (had he hit her?), and then the voices sailing from the meadow, the whipping flashlights—only that moment had weight enough to anchor the world, and make every act, no matter its scale, real.

"Oh my God," he said.

Callie rolled on her side, her body awkward and pale, and spat in the grass.

"Are you...?" he said. "Can I...?" But when he touched her she fell back shrieking.

"*Callie?*" Peter shouted.

A world that'd been anything he made of it now was a single, mute hardness. He could not, with a fingernail, scratch off the least flake.

"Callie, baby?" Peter called.

He touched her skin, or was about to, but then yanked on his shirt and sweats, his boots, and with the flashlights drawing nearer crashed off through the brush. After what seemed like hours, he came out on a beach and kicked into the river, the sweats soaking and dragging, the stones shifting underfoot. The opposite bank was steep, but he clambered up it, clawing at roots and branches. He climbed as high as he could and fell in some grass, where dew had fallen.

Far below, the two flashlights drifted lazily, like lightning bugs. They'd followed him, it seemed like, and now were drifting back. They moved along the bank until, at what must've been Callie, the beams fell from hands and snapped into cockeyed angles. Nothing in the world, Mitchell realized, no magic or mighty hand, could cancel this.

In the hours that followed, as the flashlights resumed their spirits and floated to the meadow, as the motor home's headlights sprung over the grass and swept into the road—as they wound down the canyon and, perhaps an hour later, as the other lights, the chain of reds and blues, wound up the canyon—Mitchell did have another thought. The life he'd lost, the wife. In its way, that was just as irrevocable. It was gone, but having happened it was preserved, like the moon landing and Shakespeare, in a vault of fact. It was forever, those thirteen years, those moments and glances, the afternoons returning home he'd found Bethany in the garden. She wiped her forehead and smiled at him as if for the first time. It always would be.

None of it, not a breath, would be forgiven—not a word or glance—but it was finished, Mitchell decided, and was the cost of bequeathing to history those moments in the garden. In the meadow, and downstream at what he guessed was his campsite, they'd erected floodlights. He heard the generators, and eventually dogs. He was up again, tripping and skidding to the river.

He crossed the water and passed through the cottonwoods, an army of flashlights populating the darkness around him. The floodlights reached the edge of the meadow, but no one saw him until he was halfway across. They were darkened shapes, silhouetted against the glare. One noticed him, then several whirled and were shouting. He walked on. They wanted to see his hands, were shouting for his hands, but his hands were under his shirt, as if grasping something, and would remain there.

"Show us your fucking hands!" someone shouted.

"I won't do that," he said. "It won't happen." When he did show his hands it was sudden, as were the flames stabbing the night, the moon reeling past like the scope of some physician, a grave physician seeking his gravest wounds.

AT YOUR SIDE

THEY CALLED ME LATE, at two in the morning, from the morgue. They were hysterical. Paula tried to explain, then handed the phone to John, who got through maybe a sentence before he broke down. I was out of bed, pulling on a shirt. I padded around for my collar. "Wait there," I said, though it wasn't clear who in particular was on the phone now. I heard breathing noises, and sniffling. I zipped my pants. "I'm on my way."

When I got there, a worker I'd met before, a technician, led me downstairs. We came to a steel door for which he had keys. "How've you been, Father?" he said.

"Well, thank you."

He unlocked and opened the door. "They're in pretty rough shape."

"Of course."

"I guess you know what you're doing."

He stepped aside, and I walked past him down a tiled hall. At the end of it, in some chairs, were Paula and John and their other son, whose name I didn't remember. He was younger, maybe seventeen. They stood when they saw me, but I waved them down. "Sit, sit." When they were seated, I knelt and gathered their hands. "We're going to pray."

When that was finished, I opened my eyes. I patted their knees and wrists.

"Father?" John said.

"What is it?"

"We…" He drew a breath, but couldn't go on. Paula tried to speak, but it was their son who found words. "You have to do it," he said.

"Pardon?"

"Tommy…" his mom said.

"He does. That's why he's here."

I understood what they wanted. "I'll do it," I said.

"You're sure?" Paula said.

"Wait here."

I moved down the hall and rapped at the door. It's more common than you'd think, the family making this request. They can't do it themselves, but can't leave their parent, or in this case their son and brother, alone in there. Someone I didn't know opened the door and stepped aside. I walked past her into different light, different tile. "Over here," she said, and led me to one of the tables, where she folded back the sheet. There he lay, Matthew Alden Edwards, twenty-six years old. "That's Matt," I said.

"Heart attack," the woman said.

"It's sad."

"Something could show in the tests, but…" She shook her head.

"His heart stopped."

"I'm afraid so."

I watched him there. He didn't look unfamiliar, except for the thickened quality the dead assume. It was the face I'd seen every week since he was a boy (he'd kept coming to Mass, long after his family had stopped). I'm not sure how I missed the tattoos. There was the sheet, I guess.

"Father?"

I took the oil from my pocket and anointed him, and said the prayers. "Okay," I said, and went back to the family. They stood again, as if expecting news, though of course it was news they'd already heard.

In my office in the morning, I brewed coffee and waited. There were no appointments, but the Edwards family would be along. They had to be. After a death, there were things to see to.

While waiting, I started on my side of things. I took a notepad from the drawer and swung my heels onto the desk. Beyond the window of that office was a wide lawn and trees. It was a nice office. I still think about it. For a while, I tapped a pen on my lip. Then I remembered a day after Mass I'd walked with Matt to his car. It'd been winter, one of those weak-lighted days. We'd walked to his car. It wasn't much of a story, but recalling it, picturing Matt with his hands in his coat pockets, I had the impression of a soft-spoken, careful young man who listened well. Those were good qualities, reserve and attentiveness, so I wrote them down. *Matt was soft-spoken and observant. He rather would hear what you had to say than speak himself...*

I'd started expounding on that, explaining what we could learn from Matt's example, when a door opened down the hall. Thursday morning in a rectory you heard every little noise. I slipped the notepad in its drawer and crossed the office. I opened the door just as John knocked. "Come in," I said, "please." It was the three of them. I showed them to the sofas and poured coffee.

We sat awhile before anyone spoke. That was fine. In its earliest hours, death is raw. Before even attempting speech we know instinctively it will fail, know the event will defy our efforts at structuring it. Time must pass before we talk things into place.

Paula watched her hands. "Father," she said.

"I'm listening."

"We want to thank you for last night. Or this morning. God, this morning..."

"It's not necessary."

"Because we don't...well, you know."

"Please."

"We don't go to Mass."

"I was glad to come."

We sat with our coffee. The brother stared in his mug as if looking in a pit.

"Well," Paula said finally. "I guess we're here about a service."

"We'll discuss that, absolutely. However," I set my coffee on the table, "if it's all right, I'd like to discuss Matt. That should come first."

The kid's eyes lifted.

"Matt?" Paula said.

"Yes."

"What would you like to know?" said John.

"It's not anything I want to know. Our job is mourning your son. We should consider his memory."

"Why?" the kid said.

"Pardon?"

"You didn't know him."

"Thomas," his father said.

"I knew him some. Not as well as I'd have liked. That's where you can help me."

The kid was about to say something, then didn't.

"Is that acceptable?" I said.

He was silent.

"What I'd like is if each of you shared your connection with Matt, your own experiences."

"I'm not doing this," the kid said.

"Thomas…"

"He doesn't have to, that's okay." When there were no other objections, I gestured at John. "Would you start?"

John shifted in his chair. Finally he said, "Matt was a good kid. He didn't get into trouble. I think he had things he liked. You know, he worked with his hands. We'd get him two-by-fours, things like that. He'd make things, birdhouses. He made these boxes with sliding tops."

"That's right," Paula said.

John gazed at the air before him.

"What else?"

"He never hurt people. You know, he was happy with himself. That was enough. He didn't need…" His hand fluttered. "What am I trying to say?"

"He was gentle," Paula said.

"Gentle," John agreed. "That's how I'll remember him."
Then he said, "God, remember him. Suddenly we're remembering."

"Paula, what about you?"

She had her answer ready. "Matt was easy to talk to. That's
what I remember. He'd sit with you. You know a lot of people
won't sit with you. They want to be somewhere else. He'd sit for
hours. He was comfortable."

"What else?" I said.

She thought about it. "He was considerate. Other people
came first. You know there was this Christmas…"

She told a story about Matt at Christmas. Their elderly
neighbor, proud, had declined offers to shovel his walk, and so
Matt had done it at night, while the man slept.

"That's wonderful," I said.

"He never said a word about it."

"Thomas, do you remember this?"

When the kid didn't reply, his father said, "Son, Father asked
you a question."

But he didn't speak, not then and not for the rest of the
meeting. We told other stories (I talked about walking Matt to his
car), then discussed arrangements. Services would be Saturday. As
the family wasn't religious, there'd be no Mass or vigil, just a liturgy.
The kid stared at his coffee.

Rather, he spoke one other time. They'd stood to leave.
"What about his halo?" he said.

"Pardon?"

"Matt's halo. Be sure it fits in the box."

I didn't, and still don't know what I could've said to that. John
took his son's arm. "Let's go."

More than an orator or counselor—more even than a minister—a
priest is a writer. Like a writer, we encounter him only in his
product, while his toil of production remains hidden. That's what

the week's for. There was a joke I had with other clergy. On the first day, God created priests, pens, and coffee. A week later, He sat in the pew and waited.

After the Edwards' departure, I sat in my office with the notepad. There was a way I wrote funeral homilies (not to be confused with eulogies), a form I trusted. It began with extolling the departed, and his spirit. After that, I encountered the loss. I acknowledged the pain of it, and mystery. Finally, I affirmed who the departed had been. Loss notwithstanding, there was a way he'd lived. The line I closed with, or rather the sentiment for which, each new occasion, I found alternate phrasing, was: What happened once happens still, and happens forever. A man's life lies like soil in the Earth, recorded indelibly on the ledger of time.

I wrote, *Friends and family, loved ones gathered here today. Missing from our number is a gentle individual, a young man who'd give his ear sooner than words. Who, as his mother shared with me, would sit with a person, and dwell without embarrassment in the rooms of that person's heart. We think back on Matt, and on the example he set...*

If I may, it was an eloquent beginning. I'd presided, of course, over hundreds of funerals, and in that beginning was the just-formalized syntax and somber tone the occasion demanded. It offered lofty, while not overly lofty, sentiment, the kind that stirred hearts faintly, without the hearts knowing it. It was solid. Only when I tried to write more—when I pressed pen to page and tried to add words—I stalled. I waited, but nothing came. Then, like Lot's wife (though I had to be careful thinking in such terms—nothing deflated a sermon like Biblical references), I looked back. And while it all was there, the syntax and sentiment, the subtle grandiloquence, the words I'd written were flimsy.

I read them again, and again. As any writer will attest, the first step of revision is denial. Something is missing, but you want it not to be and so read it into the text by force. This fails, of course, yet you keep at it. If you're a man of endurance (as are most men who spend thirty years in the clergy), you might keep at it forever, and never concede the thing's absence. But after maybe an hour, I sighed and held the notepad differently, to see the words anew. What was needed wasn't there.

I crossed out what I'd written, and wrote instead, *Loved ones gathered here today, there is no higher virtue than opening your life, unreservedly, to others. What we had in Matt, while we had him, was a man with that gift. Visiting this week with his mother, I learned…*

But this time, even writing I felt the flimsiness. I dropped the pen and gazed out the window. It was midafternoon. The trees, which that morning had been dewily fresh, were parched and ugly. One of my favorite writers at the time was Hemingway. That always surprises people—we assume a priest's favorite writers are C.S. Lewis, Thomas Aquinas, and Flannery O'Connor, in that order. But I liked Hemingway, who was known for writing one true sentence at a time, just one sentence, as a method of moving forward. So I tried that. I crossed out what I'd written, drew a breath, and wrote:

Matt Edwards was peaceful, and welcomed others into his heart.

That was solid. It was a truth to which a second truth, a second sentence, might be added. But then I read the sentence again, and it was hollow.

By evening, the notepad was flayed and lay on the floor like a dead bird. I'd opened a fresh pad, but it was going poorly. Worse than hollow, the words I wrote were obvious. They were transparent. This especially was troubling, as to be transparent a thing fails at concealment. Until reading those failed sentences, I'd not realized I was concealing anything. Yet there it was.

I scratched out my words and began again. The sun flattened in the window and climbed the walls. Soon, I had another dead bird.

When I should've noticed Matt's skin—noticed and warned the family, though I've never regretted not warning the family, I only regret not noticing—was the following afternoon when I visited

Larsen and Sons, who were preparing the remains. Witnessing the preparation isn't an official duty. To my knowledge, nothing is written about it. But the mortician's work always struck me as holy, and integral to our celebration of the deceased. It's the mortician, after all, who inherits our Earthly dust, and is charged with reviving it, if only marginally, so that life might once more be glimpsed in lifeless matter. Really, he does with sutures and rouge what the homilist does with words. He's an arm of the homily, and so it was fitting I take an interest.

Roger Larsen worked out of his home, which also had been the home his father worked out of, and grandfather. He answered the door in tweed slacks, like an ordinary man, which of course he was. "Father!" he said.

"Roger."

"Come in."

We'd known each other for years, and respected each other's work. We served the same families, in the same moments of need, and had in common the challenges of that service. Before seeing to the remains, we sat in his study and drank coffee.

"The poor kid," he said.

"It's a tragedy."

"You never like this work. We've talked about this. You're proud you do it, but you don't like it. Then you get a kid." He shook his head.

"I can't imagine."

"He was twenty-six, Bill. My son's twenty-six. They knew each other from school."

"You do important work, Roger."

"Well."

We discussed other things. The coffee finished, Roger led us down the hall, the rooms carpeted and softly lighted, until we passed into a clinical area, where the floor was tile and the light stringent. Matt, naked, lay on a table near some instruments. As I've said, Roger and I'd worked together many times. He understood, and I think appreciated, my coming there. And so, graciously, he bowed his head while I prayed over him. The prayer was simple. I asked that the Lord's grace pervade his hands, and assist in his sanctified work. "Amen," I said, and he said it too. Roger himself was Catholic.

My prayer for the body was equally simple. I asked that the Holy Spirit make of this flesh a fitting repository for human love, first for the care of Roger, and then for the grief of a family. May our flesh accept in death the love that while living sustained it. In any case, that was the prayer I said over bodies, the prayer I made a practice of saying. That day, over that body, I couldn't manage it.

I stood at the table.

"Father?" Roger said.

I had words. They lay on my tongue. But even prior to utterance, I felt about my prayer what I'd felt the previous evening, struggling with my homily. In this case, the words themselves weren't false. Prayer, after all, cannot be false. It merely expresses longing, without aspiring to truth. Rather it was the act. It was a false act, beautifying the deceased. We'd not even started (Roger had just snapped on a glove), but already we'd encountered all a person ever knew of death: a corpse. Beyond that, everything was evasion.

"We okay?" Roger said.

I said the prayer, but it felt ugly. Then I stepped away, and Roger began. The embalming was finished, but he arranged caps in Matt's eyes and sutured them closed. He opened the mouth and pressed in cotton, and began the mandible suture. He fed a needle under the tongue, then pressed so that the needle elongated, like some time lapse of a growing whisker, from Matt's chin.

Thinking back, I see them there, under the lamp. I even see myself seeing them. They were tattoos, and not discreet ones, either. They began at his hands and snaked up his arms. One was fingers gripping his neck, while another, on his shoulder, was a spear. How I couldn't have noticed them, and realized their importance, is baffling. I suppose I was tired. I'd been up most of the night.

In any case, they were there to see. I even saw them, however blindly, before looking away.

I waved at Roger. "I'll see you."

"You taking off?"

"I've got to finish the service."

The next morning, wearing my stole, I left through the side of the church, and in the fenced garden between the church and rectory smoked a cigarette. It'd been years since I'd smoked, though I'd smoked regularly as a seminarian. Everyone had. The joke was it was about celibacy. We were finished with sex, why not light up? Though the real reason, naturally, was nerves. We were giving our first homilies then, which was a daunting responsibility. I suppose, that morning, I'd reacquired those seminarian nerves. I'd not finished Matt's service. Rather I'd finished it, but in a hackneyed flurry sometime after 2 a.m., scrawling out every platitude I could muster. Matt was gentle, kind, giving, humble, gentle again, on and on. It was shameful, but at least I'd finished it, and it lay inside on the lectern. Through the fence I heard relatives arriving, car doors slamming and hushed, sympathetic greetings. They lingered on the church steps, perhaps wondering who was smoking.

Before an altar boy could discover me, I snuffed the cigarette in a birdbath and went inside. The service was starting. That was the bad news. The good news was I'd just do it. That's what I'd decided. I knew how funerals went. I'd do it, and it'd be over.

I met the pallbearers on the sidewalk and shook hands. They had my profoundest sympathy. One of them, it turned out, was Thomas. "My condolences," I told him, and shook the next hand down. Roger opened the car, and they withdrew the casket. "This way," I said.

In the vestibule, with my back to the congregation, I sprinkled the casket with water from my aspergillum. What a tool that'd been, my aspergillum, what a tool and what a word (the Church, I believe still, is a reliquary for our finest language). The casket blessed, I preceded it down the aisle. The congregation stood. Led by Evelyn, our cantor, we sang "Be Not Afraid." That was a hymn you sang at funerals. It was standard. Still, approaching the altar, singing, *Be not afraid / I go before you always*, I admit I was touched. I was something, in any case. Behind me lay a boy who'd probably been afraid when his chest seized, and who at his final remembrance had only me to go before him. On top of which something else was happening. I didn't know it, but I myself was departing. Like Matt, I was going somewhere, without knowing where and without, as we hear in the hymn, knowing the way.

I assumed the altar and faced those assembled. The pallbearers withdrew, at which point Roger and Scott oriented the casket. Funeral liturgies don't always include a viewing, and had this one been omitted perhaps things would've been different. But there's only the way things happen, and not how they might've happened, and along the course of that happening are we swept, without rudder. Roger lifted and locked the lid. There, on his back, lay Matt.

We were seated. Someone, I believe a cousin, read from Isaiah, after which we heard from Thessalonians. When it was time, I assumed the lectern and delivered the gospel, then seated the congregation and began my remarks.

"Matthew," I said, and let his name hang in the rafters. I dimmed an eye as if conjuring his spirit, "…was the sort of individual with whom we're not often enough blessed. And when so blessed, in those rare instances, the moment's always fleeting. How couldn't it be? How much time, in this young man's company, would've been enough? He was twenty-six. Far too young. But had this day come sixty years from now, as we all agree it should've—even then we wouldn't have had our fill."

Heads were nodding. Handkerchiefs dabbed at eyes. This was what they wanted, so I drew breath and prepared to give them the rest of it. It was then I glanced at the front pew.

In thirty years, I'd seen dozens of grieving mothers. They looked a certain way in their pews, and if Paula at that moment arrested my attention it was because she deviated so sharply from the type. She wasn't gazing at Matt the way bereaved mothers gazed (that vacant, desiccated gaze you saw once and knew forever). Rather, she was engaged in study. It was as if Matt were a puzzle. Then, as I watched, her study resolved into something sharper.

I went on, "In Matt we found tranquility, an outward calm testifying to inner peace. His steady hand was his steady heart..."

But she was out of the pew, murmurs rippling through the church, and approaching the body.

"Paula?" John said. "Hon?" He made to stand, but didn't. Slowly, as if entranced, she craned her neck, studying her son sideways.

I bent the microphone away. "Paula?"

"What is this?" she said.

"Paula," I said, "sit down."

She was still, then reached in the casket and touched Matt's chin. There was commotion in the church. "Paula?" I said.

"What's on his neck?"

"Take your seat."

She raised her voice, "God, and his hands. What'd you do to him?"

"John?"

Her husband got to her and tried to lead her back, but she pushed him off. "What is this?" she demanded.

"Paula, sit down," I said. Other people had stood, their hands ready as if to assist. They didn't know what to do.

"*What'd you do to him?*"

Roger stepped forward.

"*You,*" she said.

"Mrs. Edwards..."

John tried again to pull her back, but she broke free and once more reached in the casket. She wrenched up Matt's arm and yanked back his sleeve. "You tell me what this is!" she screamed. The hand was stiff, as if Matt were waving hello.

John pulled her away, and the hand fell.

"Shut it," I said.

Roger looked at me helplessly.

"Shut the lid."

He moved to the casket and slid the lock from the hinge. That lowered part of it. "Do you want...?" he said.

"All of it. Shut it."

He closed the casket.

Into the microphone, I said, "Okay, please. Everyone."

The congregation glanced around, pooling their astonishment.

"Everyone, please. Take your seats."

Eventually, the room settled. Paula, again in her pew, wept softly while John rubbed her back.

If you can believe it, we finished the service. I found where I'd left off. "It was a steady heart. Matt had a steady heart," I said, and took it from there. Quality by quality, like so many bricks, I reconstructed the Matt we'd agreed on, walling over the Matt who just then had waved at us. Because that hadn't happened. That'd been...no, we all agreed. That wasn't so.

In closing, I said, "Friends. What overwhelms us about death, what truly wounds us, is its permanence. We'll not see Matt again. But there's another permanence. Let us remember that. A man's life, his hours of living. That merges with eternity. Like any fact, it's imperishable. Even now, Matt has joined forever the realm of true things, which we know is the realm of God."

After which, we said the Prayers of the Faithful.

The recessional that day was "Pie Jesu." Evelyn—whom I've wondered about, I don't know what's become of her—had a wonderful, glassy soprano. The pallbearers stepped forward and assumed their handles. We went out into daylight.

It was in the car—I rode with the family, in procession behind the dark wagon—that I thought of Matt, alone in that wagon, behind glass and curtains, behind his suit, his knotted tie—thought of Matt and knew I'd not do it again. Not the funerals, none of it. How lonely he must've been. Those inner rooms. Some shade of himself, some refraction, had reached skin, but what could that tell us? Only that more lay where language couldn't touch it. Not his own language, certainly not ours. This isn't news. From our earliest hour, observing our own infant fist, we know life beats invisibly within. It's only later, and for me was much later (in the rearview mirror of John's car, I was an old man), we realize it remains so, that our hearts are small packages delivered not to the world, nor to other people, but, at the appointed hour, to silence. I was sorry, and am sorry still. *Matt*, I should have said in the homily, *we're sorry*.

At the cemetery, near a blue canopy, was a concealed mound of dirt. The cars circled, the whole long procession. We parked, and John and Paula crossed the grass.

"It was his tats," Thomas said from the backseat.

"I understand."

"She didn't know."

When I didn't say anything, he said, "What now?"

"What do you mean?"

"Should we do something?"

I've thought a great deal about Matt's funeral, about what I said and what it failed to mean. But what I told his brother, I believe, was true.

"You'll wish you'd known him," I said.

We watched his family abandon their cars, and converge at a grave.

FLAMINGO MOTEL

YOU WOULDN'T BELIEVE THIS FLIGHT TO SPOKANE. Pasco to Spokane. That's 50 miles. They have a plane for 50-mile flights. I'd have driven it, except I'd been Bangkok–Tokyo–San Fran–Pasco, and I'd been drinking. I'd still have driven it, if I'd wanted to, but I hadn't. 50 miles. The plane was a dildo you sat on. I guess you sit on every dildo, but still. It was insulting to board this thing. I'm not even tall. I'm respectably tall, I'm 6'1", but boarding this plane I was bent at the waist like I was kowtowing, and I don't kowtow, even when returning from Asia. Where was my seat? the stewardess wanted to know. I don't know, maybe it was one of the six seats in the airplane. There was one other passenger. Maybe I was sitting where they weren't. Christ, I hate people. I hate how they think. 50 miles, pure turbulence, and no booze.

No one knew I was coming. Mom, Dad, Jess. They didn't know. This was a surprise. A month earlier my employer, Anders Stern, had restructured and flushed my pussy with severance pay. Six months' salary, no questions asked. It's not like getting fired, if that's what you're thinking. Banks restructure. It happens. Fired's when your boss at State Farm Altoona rolls back his JCPenney sleeves and asks you to join him in his corkboard cubicle. Restructured is taking your severance pay and blowing tits in Ko Chang for a month. That was me. Now I'd tacked on this visit home. Why? I don't know why. Why'd you go to public college? That was you who did that, not me.

I got not a cab in Spokane, but a car, a black Lincoln with a black guy driving it, because cabs aren't found in backwater places like Spokane and because I ride Lincolns when I go places, not cabs, even in places where cabs are plentiful, like in New York City, where I live. The driver was Lonnie. He was professional. The whole way to Coeur d'Alene, where my family lives, he maintained a dignified air. And he was a good sport when I got out of the car, saw my folks' house, and got back in. "Go," I said.

It was after midnight. Everything in the car was black, including Lonnie but excepting Lonnie's white eyes, which shone in the rearview. He eased down the block. "Where to?"

"I need accommodations."

"That's arrangeable," he said.

There's actually an acceptable hotel in Coeur d'Alene, but Jess, my sister, works in the lobby. Lonnie brought me instead to a travesty on Sherman Avenue with an actual glowing vacancy sign and pink trim that couldn't possibly have been called but was called anyway: Flamingo Motel. Not *The* Flamingo Motel. Flamingo Motel. A motel for flamingos.

Why didn't I knock at my parents' door? I was tired, I'd been in Thailand. And it's not your fucking business anyways.

I decided I'd bring cinnamon rolls for breakfast. That was the plan. My dad loves cinnamon rolls. He was a teacher before he retired, but what he needed was a teacher to teach him cinnamon rolls are dog shit. When that didn't happen, he spent his whole life loving cinnamon rolls. Now we have to feed him cinnamon rolls till he dies.

My phone informed me there was a bakery just for cinnamon rolls on Government Way. The name of the place was Stop, Drop, Cinnamon Roll. When the woman on the phone said, "Stop, Drop, Cinnamon Roll, can I help you?" I wanted to shoot myself in the face. Flamingo Motel, now this. Are the people starting these businesses not hoping for money? Is their aim dodging capital? Your business is a joke you made up. Unless it's funny when your business dies, and your family eats dog shit off the sidewalk, stop telling jokes. Come up with something real, like Anders Stern Capital Management.

I ordered twenty fresh buns. I hoped my dad wouldn't be disappointed when I only brought twenty buns for him to eat.

I told Lonnie to meet me at Stop, Drop, Cinnamon Roll. I would've met him at Flamingo Motel, except I'd spent the night at Flamingo Motel and destroyed my back on the Chinese torture robot they called a mattress, and suffered seizures from the pink walls. If I didn't walk around and lower my systolic blood pressure I was going to hang myself.

It was sunny out, and already hot, though not Thailand hot. The heat in Thailand melts your pants off for fellatio. This was just heat. The sun was a yellow circle. I walked along. In a minute, I'd have twenty cinnamon rolls for my dad's face, except what I realized, walking down Sherman, was it was eight a.m., and no way at eight a.m. was my dad not already at Stop, Drop, Cinnamon Roll stuffing his maw. It was a bakery for cinnamon rolls. Where else would he be? He'd be there, or be dead, and either way there was no reason to go. Plus I couldn't keep walking. My spine was a dick in my back. I'd bring the cinnamon rolls for lunch, I decided, which dad wouldn't object to. I called Lonnie and told him to drive around.

Good luck getting drunk at eight a.m. on a Wednesday in Coeur d'Alene, except the world, it turns out, is comprised entirely of goods and services into which money at any time can be converted, provided you have enough of it, and I do. At Sherman and 5th is the Steam Engine Saloon. The owner was on the sidewalk receiving a shipment. I said, "Where on the y-axis does cash received intersect your willingness to serve me Hayman's Gin, you asshole?" He didn't understand, but I produced currency, which he understood fine. By eight-ten, I was on the Steam Engine patio with cold Bombay (he hadn't heard of Hayman's, which about stroked me out). I was roped off from the sidewalk, just me, while the citizens of Idaho, a hundred miles from the nation of Canada, walked back and forth briskly, like it mattered.

I saw her before she saw me, which gave me time to get back under the awning, in the shadows. She was up the sidewalk, peering in shop windows. I crept back for my gin, then withdrew again to the shade. It was Jamie, no doubt about it, because no one I'd ever met stood like Jamie, with her weight on her heels, like she was about to look at the sky. Jamie LePond. We'd had a thing, and I guess a long thing, as if it mattered. Good thing I'd seen her first. We might've conversed, which would've aneurismed me. Whatever she saw in the shop windows, she got bored and kept walking. When she passed the Steam Engine, I was on a knee, tying my shoe.

Stop, Drop, Cinnamon Roll still was open, but I'd ordered the rolls four hours ago and they would be stale, or dry. They'd be whatever cinnamon rolls get when they get even shittier than they were to begin with, and my dad wears JCPenney jeans but don't feed him substandard breakfast cake. I still was at Steam Engine, but they were open now and I was surrounded by waterbrains discussing Ford F-350s. I called SDCR, talking loud enough I drowned out the whole patio, which was a favor to everyone. I said, "It's me. I ordered the rolls."

It was the same jolly bitch. She laughed. "Well all's we do is rolls. I'd say your description applies to everyone!"

"Oh God Christ," I said.

"Do you have a name?"

"I ordered the biggest one, the biggest order. The crate of cinnamon rolls. I didn't come get it. That's how you know who I am. The crate of cinnamon rolls on your table that no one has come through your door to claim, those are mine, that's the customer you're addressing, fuck me."

"Andrew?" she said.

I wanted to die. "Oh my God, can we get to the purpose of

my call? Yes, Andrew. I'm Andrew. What's your name? What's your pet's name? Do you like Ford F-350s? I didn't pick up my rolls. But this isn't an apology. You've been remunerated via debit card for that purchase, so whether I pick them up is no concern of yours. They aren't your property. This call concerns a second order. I want thirty cinnamon rolls. I'll get them later. How long will it take?"

"You sound agitated," she said.

Everything that was wrong with her saying that logjammed my brain and I couldn't speak. I pounded the table, which neighboring customers didn't like but which the Steam Engine proprietor could say nothing about because his scruples were mine now, bought and paid for.

The lady said, "We'll make ten. Add those to your twenty."

"Absolutely unacceptable."

"What?"

I collected myself. "Those are dry."

"Dry? These are fresh buns!"

"Throw them out. I own them. Discard them."

"You want thirty out of the oven? You know our baker's gone home, this could take…"

I hung up. It was hang up or die. There wouldn't be cinnamon rolls after all, but my mom loved Olive Garden. I'd bring Olive Garden for dinner. Meanwhile, I stepped over the sidewalk chain and started down Sherman. I ate at a taco truck, then called Lonnie. I didn't need transportation, I needed air conditioning and silence. I sat in the car while we idled at the curb, popping around on my phone, then told him keep the meter running, and got out.

According to public records accessible via mobile devices, Jamie LePond once more was Jamie LePond, after being Jamie Frederick. She managed a thrift store on 4th Avenue and owned a bungalow worth $152,643. I started up 4th. I noticed Lonnie following me, his car inching along while traffic zoomed past. I waved him away and he turned down another street.

4th Avenue has thrift stores everywhere, all of them with

wrist-cutter names like Thrifting Gears and Threadly Force, and all of them dog shit. The name of Jamie's was Good, Bad, Snuggly. It was a house under a tree with furniture and clothes in the yard. Waterbrains were everywhere, trying on hats and drooling. I'll never be mistaken for a waterbrain, not so long as I'm living, breathing, and on the trail of maximized fiscal utility, but for a moment I blended in. I slipped through the yard, inspecting old boots and vintage milk cans.

Jamie was inside, I gathered. I'd have to go in there. But then she appeared on the porch with a hippie in flowing skirts. They admired an armoire. I slipped behind another armoire, in the yard, and watched them through the cupboard hinges.

You're thinking I felt something, some nostalgia or something, because the college you attended emphasized easy conclusions. Let me educate you. To the cultivated, there's an interest in lives not lived. Understand? An *interest*. We're not talking puppy-dog shit. I have an aquarium at home with heterochromus cichlids, Neptune groupers, and yes, a peppermint angelfish. It's in the wall in my condominium because I can afford it, and because marine life fascinates me. Sentiment's not an issue. If someone, using the Masai spear on my wall, stabbed the tank so the fish poured out and died I wouldn't care except for the angelfish, which cost $35,000, though nor would I care about the angelfish because 35k is insignificant. Understand? Jamie LePond was entertainment.

The hippie couldn't afford the armoire. Anyone could see that. They went inside, and after a while I followed.

It was like a gypsy wagon in there. Silky things and beads drooped from the ceiling. It was musty and dark, and what couldn't have been yet certainly was Cat Stevens' "Moonshadow" played through speakers which themselves were vintage items, fat and wooden with dog-shit sound. Jamie's responsibilities, from what I could see from behind a rack of polyester trench coats, were primarily clerical. She tapped a keyboard and looked at papers. Phones rang, and over "Moonshadow" and "Peace Train" and

"Rubylove" (she played the whole album—I believe it's *Tea for the Tillerman*, or *Teaser and the Firecat*), I heard her voice. "Good, Bad, Snuggly?" she said. It was the voice she'd had before. She was a redhead and talked like one, like she'd swallowed gravel.

Though not all clerical. Customers needed help with Levi's and scarves and sewing machines, and she emerged from the counter to assist them. Their questions were inane. They couldn't find price tags, or wanted instructions for lubricating the bobbin case. Questions answered, Jamie returned to the counter. She tapped keys and looked at papers.

Olive Garden was north of town, in the wastes, and even on Wednesday was crowded. I'd ordered ahead, but couldn't say the shit from their menu. "Food," I just said, "food. For five people. Ten."

"Make up your mind," the kid said.

I nearly ate my phone. "Seven entrees. Put it in boxes. Okay, I've hit the limit of talking to you. Make the food."

I'd gotten through that, but now was in Olive Garden with waterbrains drooling on my shoes and was ready to nail my belt to a fake Tuscan roof beam and swing like a wind chime. The hostess had empty, zoo-animal eyes and couldn't understand my words. "Food," I said. "Food, food. I ordered...on the phone. Your colleagues are making it or it's made already. Your function is bringing it here."

"This is dine-in or to-go?" she said, and something popped in my eye. It was leave Olive Garden or decease from the Earth. Luckily, Lonnie had the common touch. I waited in the car while he got the food, then we drove to my parents' house.

The food was unevenly heated, though, and seeping through the cardboard. Plus it was contained in cardboard, for Christ's sake, and stank like dog shit. I peeled the foil off one of the boxes. It looked like pig guts in there. I rolled down the window and got my face in the wind, but it didn't help.

"You good?" Lonnie said.

"Turn around," I said.

He did, and I threw the food on someone's lawn.

Back at Flamingo Motel, I ate Tums and pretzels and drank Heineken from the gas station. To even out, I popped a Celebrex and called Lane Bergman from Trinity Group. Lane and I went to Kellogg together, which is Kellogg School of Management, which you probably think is a training program for shift supervisors at cereal factories.

"Berg," I said.

"My man."

"How closely do you follow me? You follow me."

"I know this and that."

"You follow me. Shut up."

"I'm aware you got axed."

"Please."

"No?"

"One seventy-five for cleaning out my desk? Axe me any day, if that's getting axed."

"They made you clean your desk?"

"Fuck no. Okay, this is boring. What've you got?"

"For you?"

"Come on, say it, say it, say it."

Berg sighed. He likes flirting around and not saying meaningful shit, which is why he won't rise over VP, though he doesn't know that yet. "For you, we're looking at junior portfolio management. But there's a spot."

"Junior? Fuck you."

"You were a junior at Anders!"

"I had acne as a kid, that doesn't mean I want more!" (Which was rhetorical, I never had acne.)

"You want the interview?"

I uncapped a Celebrex and tapped it in my Heineken. "Yeah, give me the interview." That really was why I'd called, just to get my name on the books. I wouldn't work at Trinity, because Trinity's dog shit. Where I'm working next is Gillman Shaw. The phone call was to waste Berg's time.

I needed to acclimate, all right? You couldn't hit Coeur d'Alene and see your family immediately. The pressures needed to equalize, like when you scuba dive in St. Maarten or fly into La Paz, Bolivia at 12,000 feet, not that you'd know.

I ate breakfast at some dog-shit place because to acclimate I needed exposure to dog-shit things. Beyond that, all I needed was time. I sat on the patio, sipping what they called a Bloody Mary.

After breakfast, I walked down Mullan, which is a street for poor people. The sun was in the trees, while these cheap, screw-on-your-hose sprinklers hissed water on dinky lawns. Some kid had parked her bike on a sprinkler, so all the sprinkler watered was her pedals, which was idiotic because bikes and cheap sprinkler heads both are ambulatory devices, either of which is perfectly effective when ambulated clear of the other, and perfectly dog shit when not, yet there they were. The thing in my eye was popping again. There were no cars in the street. The $152,643 bungalow was a blue box at the corner of Mullan and 17th.

Across the street was a house either abandoned or occupied by derelicts, the shrubs overgrown and yard weedy. I slipped through the weeds, the dew staining my Cucinelli flat-fronts, which luckily were my old Cucinellis, but which even if they were my new ones weren't irreplaceable for a man of my means. I parted the bushes and watched. A back door opened and slammed shut, and an old dog, a Wirehaired Vizsla, nosed out and peed in the yard. I hadn't remembered Jamie had a Viszla, but this was it, this was the dog. Herb. Herb was a puppy when I'd known him, and had ruined most of my shoes, though the shoes I'd worn then had deserved eating by Vizsla. His pee was difficult. Nothing came, and eventually he couldn't keep his leg up. He squatted there, then fell in the grass.

I walked around, and cut back through the alley. From the

garage, or what in Jamie's neighborhood passed for a garage, I saw through the kitchen window. She sat at the table with a box of cereal, generic brand, and a book balanced against a milk carton. As I watched, she slopped bite after bite, milk dribbling onto her Tweety Bird pajamas. Her hair was insane, little flaps and wings of it sticking every direction.

The other window was her bedroom, where a lamp was on. I saw her bed with its scattered pillows, and behind that an armoire no doubt purchased, at an embarrassing employee discount, from Good, Bad, Snuggly. Hung over the armoire door were dresses and jeans, and farther back, on the walls, I made out secondhand knickknacks, paper balloons and such. To make their tastes seem thoughtful, rather than impoverished, the poor sometimes tack trash to their walls.

A car appeared up the alley. To make it seem I lived there, I inspected the garage's siding, as if later, after a day at the jobsite, I'd make repairs and drink malt liquor in the yard. But as was obvious to anyone, I didn't and couldn't live there. I wore Cucinellis. Even the soggiest waterbrain differentiates Cucinellis from the pants he himself can afford, even stained Cucinellis, to say nothing of the intrinsic qualities that set me apart organically, Cucinellis or no. Plus the garage didn't have siding. I jumped the fence, leaving a scrap of Cucinelli where anyone could find it, and ran down the side of the building.

When the car had passed, I peeked around at the house. Jamie was at the table, but as I watched she carried her bowl to the sink. It was eight o'clock, according to my Breguet Classique (yellow gold with up-shaded crocodile band)—time for work. She shook grounds in her coffeemaker, and filled the carafe with water from the tap. I mentioned my fishes, my aquarium. The gay man, Leonard, who advises my aquarium decisions, always emphasizes context, *context*. Aquarium accouterments, the flora and coral beds, aren't—and Leonard says the word with such gay-man disdain—*decorative*. They're your comprehension of the fish. They're what endow the fish, and its habits (he likes to connect "habit" to "habit-at," but it's strained rhetoric and when he deploys it I ignore him), with meaning. And so watching Jamie, I knew not to watch Jamie, but the blue hut she moved through, one window to the next. Also I watched her yard, with its clothesline and patio furniture, the sun in the trees, the cars passing in the street, the neighbor's sprinkler wetting my pant cuff. That was Jamie's context, her aquarium, and there she was, swimming. As with any aquarium, it was closed off, and yet a complete world unto itself, whole and safe. I mention this not because it's important, but because you attended a land-grant university and probably think I was getting emotional, watching my ex move through her life, watching the space of that life surround her. But look: I felt nothing watching Jamie that I don't feel most mornings watching Clementine, my peppermint angelfish, peck motes off her mushroom coral, and when I'm bored of that I go to the office and manage stacks.

She went in the bathroom, so I circled the house for a better vantage. A car appeared at the corner, so I knelt and studied the grass, until the car drove on (perhaps the most profitable thing you learn about lesser minds is they defer automatically to anyone engrossed in detail). I was about to move again when Herb came around the house. He knew I was there but couldn't find me, the blind fucker. He sniffed the air, trustful and sleepy like all blind things, though I'm not sure he smelled much either, old as he was. He amounted to crust and joints, and nothing more. What seemed at first just instability, a kind of rickety swaying, actually was his wagging tail. He whined softly. "Herbert," I whispered, though he just swayed and whined. I went over and he licked my hand. He tried to stand his paws on me, by which means he'd ruined several of my suits, years ago, but couldn't lift his feet.

He fell in the grass again. So as not to arouse the neighborhood's suspicion, I screwed off the sprinkler head and gave the spigot a turn. Spraying the eave back and forth (poor people always hose down their houses), I side-stepped, step by step, toward the bathroom window. I heard the shower, and her voice. She wasn't singing so much as mumbling a song, or murmuring. Beneath her voice was the click of things—a snapped shampoo cap and dropped razor, the shower curtain skating down the rod. I sat beneath the window. So she wouldn't hear it, I trained the hose wide of the house, the water arcing through the sun.

I could see in, if just barely. The curtain was no more than gauze. And close as I was, I felt steam wafting out. It dampened my skin, then evaporated. On the steam was the scent of soap and some fruity conditioner, and more generally the scent of entering a bathroom while a woman showers there, knowing a warm and slippery thing waits in the fog. Softening my focus, I saw the form of her on the curtain, her face upturned. I watched till she killed the water, then listened while she dried her hair.

One less profitable thing you learn about lesser minds is they demand explanations for phenomena they've observed, while refusing to entertain the possibility they've observed them poorly, which of course they have. My sister, for a job, stands in a hotel lobby wearing a pantsuit. By all indications, she realizes this about herself. Yet her confidence in her own deductive powers remains unshaken.

The carelessness was my fault. While acclimating to Idaho, I should've been more deliberate about staying out of sight. The only place I could stay out of sight was Flamingo Motel was the problem, and if I spent another hour in that pink shop of horrors I ran the risk of staying all the way out of sight forever, in that I'd smash the mirror and use a glass shard to cut ruts in my ulnar and radial arteries. Instead, I took some Heinekens under the tree by the sidewalk. There was a picnic table there. It was chained to the trunk of the tree, which was enough to go back inside and dig for those arteries, but I hung on. I was drinking my Heinekens when Jess walked by.

"Oh my God," she said.

"Oh, shit."

"Are you here? Are you fucking here again?"

"Jessica, keep walking."

"How long have you been here?"

The recipe for a stroke is dealing with someone drawing false conclusion after false conclusion, hopping one to the next like a frog on lily pads, until they've lost touch entirely with their original, waterbrained assumption, the error of which they'd have to understand before they understood anything.

"What's this, what're you doing?" she said.

I was twitching. When each of your nerves leaps to correct a separate, untenable idiocy, you twitch.

"Look." She gazed down the street, as if I were the one requiring patience. "You gonna see Mom and Dad?"

"Listen..."

"Yes or no?"

"The world doesn't hinge on any one simplistic event. That's the first thing you should learn."

"What're you talking about?"

"Oh my God."

"It's all a travesty with you. Everything. Look, Mom and Dad. Are you going to see them?"

"If what you need to comprehend the world..."

"This is ridiculous."

"Jess, if what you need is the declaration that some single event will transpire..."

"Can you hurry this up?"

Her mind, her rodent mind, would not be still. "Yes. Okay, yes. Is that what you need? Or no, if you need that."

"Bet you don't," she said.

That's fine, too."

"Are you okay?"

"Holy shit," I said.

"You're right, forget it. Look, see Mom and Dad. Okay, I'm

late." She started off, but then stopped and looked at Flamingo Motel. "Are you staying here?" Then she said, "You know what, forget it. Look, take care of yourself. Jesus." As she walked up the street, I heard her say, "Can't believe you're fucking here."

I'm not one of these people who make mistakes repeatedly, like a lab hamster always sucking the electrified waterspout. I don't make mistakes period, but when I do I make them once and thereafter am correctly wired. To avoid further detection, I had Lonnie drove me to JCPenney. I couldn't go in, of course, but gave him money so he could purchase me shitty clothes.

Before going in, he said, "How you doin' on size?"

It wasn't a difficult question. "Forty-one with fifteen collar, slim. Thirty/thirty-three, medium rise, snug lap."

He laughed.

"What?"

"You a medium. How 'bout kicks, 8 wide?"

"That's not funny."

When he was through laughing, I told him my real size. He walked off, twirling his keys.

The clothes he selected reflected the tastes of his culture, though poor people the nation over had adopted those tastes, so as a disguise it was effective. In addition to the jeans and shirt (he'd said emphatically I was a medium, yet returned with 36/36 Dickies and a 2XL Rocawear tee), he purchased a Pirates hat, embarrassing sunglasses, and vintage Reebok pumps. He stood in the parking lot of Flamingo Motel while I went in the room and changed. When I emerged, I of course looked like dog shit. But Lonnie, sipping his coffee, nodded. "You a steely motherfucker," he said.

According to my phone, Good, Bad, Snuggly closed at seven, and so at six Lonnie dropped me across the street, at Ron's Lounge. He drove off, though I had the feeling he stayed nearby, maybe around the corner. Ron's was dog shit. My chair on the patio, the chair and table both, rocked like canoes. I was motion-sick. But the costume worked. People treated me like trash, which is to say as their equal. And I could see across to Good, Bad, Snuggly. Most of the big stuff, the armoires and dressers, had been taken inside.

At six-thirty, a Nissan parked at the curb and two women in what looked like bank attire (by which I mean the attire you'd wear to your job at the Kroger branch of Wells Fargo, and not your job at Goldman or Credit Suisse, for which you'd wear immaculate virgin wool) got out and went in. At six-forty-five, which is the time at which unscrupulous employees close a shop that closes at seven, they came onto the porch with Jamie, who locked the door. They started down 4th, and I followed.

The restaurant they chose was Tacos del Fuego. My seat at the bar was near enough I heard their conversation, and the crunch of their chips. When they ordered margaritas I ordered one myself, though they didn't specify a tequila and asked for theirs blended, which Rocawear or not simply isn't the caste I belong to. Still, the four of us enjoyed a drink together. I was at their table, more or less, except with my back turned.

"Man, I'm needing this," Jamie said.

"Yeah?" her friend said.

"This hasn't been my week. You get those weeks?"

"There's other kinds?"

They laughed like idiots. They laughed loud enough I managed to say, at nearly full volume, "Play *Teaser and the Firecat.*"

"Is this related to, uh...?" her friend asked.

"No."

"Liar."

"It isn't," she said. "I'm done with him."

"Well, but there's done with him and done with him."

"I've just been edgy. I don't know. Tonight, though. Let's get after it."

"That's right."

I heard glasses clink.

"Bet you call him, though."

"I won't call him!"

"Not saying you want to call him. There's just…pressures. People need people."

"I'm looking forward, bitch."

"Oh, I know. It's just midnight rolls around…"

"Eat your chips," Jamie said, and they laughed.

"Eat your chips, bitch," I said.

Their food came, Jamie's fajitas hissing like, and about as appetizing as, a pit of snakes. I paid, and crossed the street to a coffee shop. Dusk was falling, the air heavy and blue. Whilst drinking dog-shit espresso, I watched them in the bright window of Tacos del Fuego. My phone buzzed. It was Gabe Muntz, my guy at Gillman. *Hit me tomorrow*, the message said. *Got something for you.* Who in that shitty place would've suspected Reebok Pumps was about to be Senior Strategic Analyst at a top-three equities group? Well, they couldn't see what was in front of them. That's why they were miserable. Dinner was over, and Jamie and her friends were collecting purses.

The bar they chose, if economic actors in such narrow markets can be said to choose anything, was Chirps on Sherman, which was a lightless den of misery, upholstered in dark velvet that further drained the light. Budweiser in hand, because the costume had to be thorough, I dissolved in the crowd. Walking my laps, or sitting on stray stools, thumbing my phone, I was a thread in the cloth Jamie and her friends swaddled in. I stood down the bar while they ordered blue drinks that arrived in toilet bowls.

Later, they played darts with some bottom feeders dressed exactly like me, except my shit was fresh. I stood near the darts, at a pinball machine. Behind the shades Lonnie'd purchased (wearing dark shades in dark bars is a pastime of the working class), I could stare directly at them, while only seeming to attend the little flippers and ricocheting ball.

Jamie didn't like them, I could tell. But she liked something, or wanted something, just as Clementine sometimes wants something and zooms aimlessly through her kelp. One of the guys was awful, just this muscle-bound, dog-shit person. They all were, but this one guy in particular. Throwing a dart was his full range of motion. Yet he rubbed on her, and she let it stand. Then she rubbed back. They won a game and he lifted her, her arms in the air, and when he put her down his hands stayed on her hips.

I crossed to the bar for one of the toilet drinks. Your deductive powers, purchased with in-state tuition, tell you I was jealous, but let's be clear: of one thing and one thing alone do I get jealous, and that's every dollar on this dog-shit Earth not yet sequestered in my personal accounts. Got it? Waterbrains having waterbrain fun depresses me is all, and I needed liquor. I sucked down the toilet bowl and shoved it away, then went to the jukebox to play Cat Stevens. When Jamie heard it, she broke free from Donkeyman and sang her heart into a beer bottle. She looked to see who'd played the song, but I was back at the pinball machine.

She had to send Donkeyman away or go home with him, and in the end she chose wisely. He was leaving, his meathead friends slapping thumbs on phones that in their hands looked no bigger than nine-volt batteries, sending messages no doubt devoid of punctuation and using, interchangeably, *there* and *their*, *your* and *you're*, and in the end compensating for their omitted punctuation with endless snakes of exclamation points. Donkeyman pleaded with her, his hands open as if to prove he had no weapon. I could hear his voice, the whining tone of it, but luckily couldn't make out his words. What a shotgun-chewing proposition that would've been, hearing some ogre's best rhetoric on the matter of bashing Jamie's guts. I imagine his buffet-line pleas for more gravy and additional chicken nuggets were similarly insistent. In any case, she withheld. The three of them walked off like circus bears. I couldn't help myself. When they passed I dropped my phone in their path and stooped to pick it up. "Excuse me, sorry. Circusbearssaywhat. Sorry."

"What?" the guy said.

"Nothing. Hey, have a good one. You, too. Hey…" I shook their hands as they left.

Alone, Jamie and her friends dropped in a booth and sipped beers. They weren't talking. One of them saw someone across the bar and ran to him. The other went to the bathroom. Jamie sat with her beer, watching the air the way a person watches her reflection in a window, yet there was no window, just air. She took out her phone. For a moment she studied it, turning it in her hand. Finally she tapped out a message. I moved to a nearby table and watched her over the napkin holder. She tapped another message.

Her friend returned, and the phone went in her purse not quickly enough. "James…" the friend said.

"What?"

"Jamie LePond…"

"Sit down," Jamie said.

The friend did not sit down. "Did you?"

"Sit down already."

"God, you're unbelievable."

Jamie drew a breath, the long breath of someone who's been through something repeatedly. She pushed back her hair.

"Listen, you said…"

"I texted him. That's what happened. Would you deal with it, please?"

Her friend walked off.

Where she was sitting, Jamie couldn't see me. I was off to the side. But nothing happened—she did nothing and I did nothing—so that there opened between us the kind of stillness you feel on airplanes, and you especially probably feel on airplanes, in coach, with a stranger jammed next to you. You don't look at each other, but that doesn't matter. There the two of you are, with empty hands and hours of flight time ahead. It's like you should do something, you and this other person, like a pocket of time has opened just for that purpose. It's not a feeling I like, I feel trapped, and so I crossed the bar and did what I do on airplanes, which is order vodka.

The guy must've been nearby. He just was there suddenly. He was lousy, with dumb clothes and a dumb face. After no more than a drink, Jamie was through with him. She left him there, and left the bar.

I followed her up Sherman, then up Mullan, her heels clicking the sidewalk. She appeared in streetlamps and vanished again. It was a nice effect, the streetlamps, not unlike the Bridgelux LEDs Clementine swims under, though my Bridgelux frame (customized) could buy twenty blocks of municipal lighting. In the rhythm of walking it was like I swam with her, the two of us in her warm tank, though I'll remind you such feelings aren't uncommon to the collector of elegant fish.

She opened the gate and walked in her house. One by one, the lights came on. From where I stood in the street, I could see Herb sniff her hand, his body swaying. She kicked her shoes through the room. By then, I was in the yard. It was a small house, but with the lights on, at night, it looked big enough for something, I don't know what. Something more could fit there. She was on the sofa, her phone out. As earlier, she less used the phone than considered it, turning it in her hand. Then, deliberately, she tossed it. It hit the window like a bird.

Something clearly was over. An act had concluded. And yet also...I don't know. Also it was early. Not early in the evening (it actually was late), but early in the weekend, or in the summer. Somehow it was early, and though she'd thrown her phone it still was there, on the floor. There she was on the sofa. Someone could call, or ring the doorbell. I could ring the doorbell. There we'd be, Jamie and I, in her house.

I had my phone out, texting Lonnie, but then looked up the street and saw him. The Lincoln was at the curb, its clearance lights on, exhaust pooling beneath it. I stepped over the fence, and he pulled forward.

"We doing Flamingo?" he said. We were driving, his eyes sleepy in the rearview. I'd been thinking Flamingo, but decided it was late, and seeing them now would be easy. The door'd be unlocked. I'd go in the bedroom. Them sleepy, me drunk, we'd slip into conversation like old people, which they literally were, slipping into a bath. I didn't even have to say it. Lonnie turned up 15th. We passed out of downtown into the shabbier homes, the postwars and split-levels.

He slowed as we approached, slowed nearly to a stop, but I didn't have to say it then, either. We eased by, the windows dark and lawn overgrown, then accelerated.

I had clothes at Flamingo, clothes and some money, but Lonnie got on the interstate. Sixty, seventy, eighty, we flew towards Spokane, towards the airport, not a headlamp in sight. It was hours till dawn, but the sun in New York had climbed over Brooklyn. Manhattan had its face in it, its beautiful face. I called Muntz. He didn't answer, so I called again.

"Mm?" he mumbled. He was asleep.

"Muntz. Tell me about the future."

ACKNOWLEDGMENTS

Thanks to Erin McKnight and Melissa Schoeffel, for their faith in these stories and for helping breathe life into them. I'm grateful as well for the kindness and financial support of the Arkansas Arts Council and the University of Arkansas, which was indispensible. In particular, I'm grateful for the friendship and wisdom of Skip Hays, and for Davis McCombs' perseverance on behalf of his students.

Most importantly, thanks is due to my mother and father, to Joe and Erica and Louis, and even to little Alex despite my not having met him yet. Every important thing I've ever felt is a refraction of the love you all have shown me. Thanks to Alec, Eric, and Wong, my oldest pals. And thanks to Amy—you're what I needed to believe could happen.

BEN NICKOL's stories and essays have appeared in *Alaska Quarterly Review, Redivider, Boulevard, Fugue, CutBank, Hunger Mountain Online, The Los Angeles Review, Canoe & Kayak* and elsewhere, and his second book is *Adherence*, a short novel forthcoming from Outpost19 in 2016. His fiction has earned an Individual Artist Fellowship from the Arkansas Arts Council, two Baucum-Fulkerson Awards from the University of Arkansas and the 2015 Beacon Street Prize from *Redivider*, and his nonfiction has been cited as notable work in *Best American Sports Writing*. He lives in Montana and teaches at Helena College.

CPSIA information can be obtained
at www.ICGtesting.com
Printed in the USA
BVOW10s1943080217
475635BV00002B/228/P